Our Love Is Like Anime
Eïrïc R. Durändal Stormcrow

Our Love Is Like Anime
Eïrïc R. Durändal Stormcrow

GNOMO

Collection 1,001

Our Love Is Like Anime
First English edition: June 2023

(c) Eïrïc R. Durändal Stormcrow, 2023
(c) Gnomo, 2023
Edition: Eïrïc R. Durändal Stormcrow

Design and Typesetting: Eïrïc R. Durändal Stormcrow
Cover: Jensen Art Co. (jensenartofficial)

No portion of this book may be reproduced, translated, or appropriated in any way or via any means, whether electronic, mechanical, photocopy, recording, or any other data storage and reproduction system without the author's permission in writing.

Gnomo, 2023
San Juan, Puerto Rico
gnomoliterario@gmail.com

ISBN: 9798397993739

Me and my friends, we miss rock 'n' roll
I want shit to feel just like it used to.
Lana del Rey, The Greatest

Preface

There are two kinds of people in this world: those who can weather anything, gifted as they are with a solid support network, and those of us who will weather whatever we can, with what little and reduced support system we have. This is the second draft of this preface. The first went on about how there are two kinds of people in this world: those who ask permission and those who apologize, and how, in order to truly be *unleashed* as an Artist, you have to stop being either. It wasn't that grandiloquent an introduction, I promise. But now that I've finally gone online and searched "cyanide pills," the first draft seems so naïve. And of course, Google seldom disappoints (and that should be scary): First entry is Puerto Rico's online suicide prevention hotline, followed immediately by Wikipedia's "Suicide pills" article, and Cyanide Pills, the band, whose hit "Can't Get It Up," from their 2013 album *Still Bored*, was surprisingly funny and jam worthy. Highly recommended.

During the search, several terms fly around, such as "aid-in-dying," "UCLA Health," "states with *death with dignity* laws," "end-of-life care," and a rather large number of words that make no sense to me right now, but which pierce me all the same with their hooks of despair. Weird thing is that they also fill me with hope. Because there is a way. And where there is a way, there is a plan.

Things in Puerto Rico have never ever been right. But they have never been more wrong than they are now. As Donald Trump is finally arraigned, though we all know that the weight of justice will ignore him in full and somehow his evil will go unpunished, here in the colony, I am forced to decide whether to eat every day or pay the rent. And so, I eat something every other day. I see how the price of everything keeps going through the roof, and how this is affecting us. In our relationships. How we are getting sicker, and lonelier, and sadder. And how we Puerto Ricans are eating each other alive online for the stupidest reasons, but seldom see each other for real, for a hug or even a pity fuck.

On that note, I seldom see Puerto Ricans where I live anymore. Rarely. Everywhere I look, I see a damn gringo or a fucking tourist. Or people speaking in tongues, literally. Every day I resent their presence more and more, and every day it gets harder and harder to speak English to them. And every day I keep stewing in my own juices, impotent. So, even though it is one of my two vernaculars —I learned both

English and Spanish at the same time within a culturally locked and limited Jehovah's Witness household— I no longer speak it. I haven't spoken English, privately or in public, since last year. "But speak to them," one of my very few friends would say. "It's not what you say, but how you say it. Be nice." What are the nice words for "I wish I were brave enough to molotov your airbnb with your colonizing ass inside"? How do you say that without offending? How do you say, in a polite manner, "I wish you caught the new *Candida aris* and died?" Seriously, how do you communicate that nicely?

As I write this supremely disorganized and hateful introductory text, I am concerned about my husband's health. He is in physical pain all the time, in different parts of his body, for diverse reasons. He is only 6 years my senior. We have been together through hell and back for fourteen years this August. And he is my soulmate. The love of my life. Seeing your other half —because Joey is my body and soul, and I am his body and soul; we are simply *one*— suffer, and be in pain, and know that such pain is the result of medical malpractice decisions that you don't have the money to take to court, eventually kills your spirit. It drowns you in the dark depths of Despair, an ocean where you just can't see the creatures swimming around you or below. But you can feel them, tugging at you, pricking at your heart, eating at it. Daring you to close your eyes and fall asleep for a bit. I am disorganized and I wonder how close this shit is. I wonder about Switzerland, with their *Exit* program, or anywhere in Canada. I don't want to end my life in the United States. Ew.

So, this book. There are 25 stories in it. I always thought I would die at the age of 25. And one of these stories will definitely offend you —if not all— and some may even make you burn this book. So, be advised.

And please, don't burn this book. If you hate it that much, just give it away. Leave it in some public bathroom. Give it to that aunt who has always hated you. Or give it to your pastor. But give it a chance to live. Even demons deserve to live.

Our Love Is Like Anime is the culmination of a metamorphosis that, like so many things in Puerto Rico, was imposed on me by the circumstances every Puerto Rican islander and mainlander knows. It is our collective trauma and stigma. Anime —or Japanese animation— contrary to cartoons and animation from this hemisphere, does not caricaturize life, but rather renders it in all its gory violence and mirth. This is that kind of book, a fundamentally healing book. *Ubi pus ibi evacua* and all that jazz. And demons and shit.

Eïrïc
San Juan, Puerto Rico

Hair

1.

"You will eat it, and you'll say nothing. You wanted to be here anyways," my mother says to me.

She catches me looking at the chocolate cake Mariela had made during her Lifetime cookware demonstration. All the women eat contently while I discover suspicious strands of hair all over the melted frosting. Mariela had such long beautiful hair, but the chemo had started its havoc.

"You will eat it, and you'll say nothing," she repeats, "or so help me Jehovah God I'll beat you so hard you'll shit blood for a month."

I look at the hair in the chocolate, now liquid. My mother cuts a piece of the cake, and the hair just hangs in the air, covered in the molten brown thing, until it lands on the plastic plate.

"Eat it. Now."

I try to quickly identify those parts of the piece I've been given with no hair in it, but it's as if someone had thrown in a cancer patient's entire wig as an ingredient for the dessert. Curls and all. I can't take it and barf right in front of all the ladies. And the chain reaction cannot be stopped. Soon, as my vomit lay there, with the piece of cake I had dropped to the floor, with all the curls inside, the women notice they have been eating Mariela's hair. And the barf fest ensues. My mother does not vomit. She stoically takes the retching sounds, and the gargling liquid sounds as the hairy cake ejects from the painfully weak stomachs gathered that afternoon for a Lifetime cookware presentation. And when it is all done, she cross-slaps me so hard that I fall to the floor and Mrs. Livingston has to hold her hand.

"Liana, it's not his fault. Don't do this. Really, Mariela, we love you and understand what you're going through, but this is too much."

Mariela leaves crying, but it's already late. I am already covered in vomit, cake, and hair. There's no way in hell that I'll ever forgive my BITCH ASS CUNT of a mother for this.

2.

There's this bully in high school. Name's Freddy, short for Frederick Van Heusen. Nobody knows why he's at Fergusson Heights, a public school. His father owns the Van Heusen male clothing company. So, one day, at the cafeteria, dear Freddy decides to put pubic hair in my chicken noodle soup.

"Eat it. Now."

Everybody decides to fall silent and watch. I'm everyone's favorite bold and beautiful. I'm a piss poor soap opera. Or worst. A Latin telenovela.

"No."

"What did you say? Eat it!"

I turn to him and throw the contents of the soup, scalding hot with pubic hair, at his face. He grabs it with his hands and starts screaming as his head goes shameful red. They'll later say I burnt down his head and melted his hair.

An hour later, I'm at the principal's office. A lovely lady. She knows that I've been bullied. She has known for a while that I'd snap someday. She knows this is me, snapped. There will be hell to pay.

"His parents are talking about suing your family, ma'am. Also, there's the Superintendent's recommendation to expel him."

"I don't know what's gotten into him," the bitch ass cunt dares say to my face.

I spit at her.

"This is all your fault. You're a bad mother."

And before the principal can move to hold her down, the woman who gave birth to me punches me, straight to my nose, and breaks it true.

3.

My boss tells me of this awesome "gentlemen's club" on Madison Ave. He says I've been doing a great job lately and I deserve a break. He gives me *the card* and tells me to visit Holder Jones, Mr. DaCosta's secretary.

As I careen my way to the 14th floor of the iron wrought Tamera Building, I notice how even the elevator's décor reflects a much organic art nouveau. There are traces of plants everywhere, from the frescoes on the wall, to the 19th Century French posters, to even vintage absinthe ads. The elevator stops and I propel myself to the entrance of the Big One, as people in the company naturally know the CEO's office. Holder Jones looks at me, smiles, and beckons. She wears her hair in a strange bob cut, in which every single hair is straightened with keratin. A weird kind of natural wig. It looks fake. It would still look fake from an airplane.

She covers the auricular of her wireless headset.

"Congratulations, darling! It's not every day you're admitted in the club!"

"Is that a good thing?" I ask.

"It means a promotion is in your immediate future. Keep up the good work. Make us proud," she says, and then deposits a *card* in my hand, and goes back to her call, ignoring me.

I leave and decide that it's just too good of a day not to treat myself. I go to Brooks

Brothers, at the corner of Miles and Steph East. The owner knows me well. I look at the new scarves, the ones hispters would give their whole trust funds for, and decide for the blue one.

"Can I interest you in some new suits, ties, or underwear?" asks the cute guy behind the register.

"No. I'd buy the whole store, but not today."

"Fair enough. That would be $76.99."

I pay, put on the scarf, and leave the store. Outside is warm, but this scarf is not for the cold. So, I endure while I cross Miles Ave. and the whole East Gordon Park, nervously, of course, as it's also called "Spook Park" by whites who fear blacks. A guy comes from out of nowhere and follows me. His skin is pure night with stars as cold sweat and bug song in the form of his many keys jangling inside his pockets. He catcalls some anti-white or anti-gay insult. I ignore him and go inside the park restroom. He comes after me. I piss at a urinal. He just stares from his vantage point at the sink and grabs his fully erect member through his sweatpants. I lower mine to my ankles and give him a full view of my ass. He approaches, spits on his cock, and rams it in.

"Name's Jackson," he says.

"Nice to meet you, Jackson. You're killing me."

"It happens."

He smiles and batters me even harder. He cums inside, of course. By the time he's done, I have cum four times. He withdraws. His cock is bloody. He protests.

"It happens," I say and leave.

The park's exit to the north, where the rose galleria is, leads me right in front of the Madison Ave. building. I've heard all kinds of stories about this place. The orgies, the gangbangs, the constant cruising, the STDs... No clothing allowed, no rules, no holds barred. I enter. The man behind the counter asks for *the* card.

"Here."

"Alright, sir, please enter the elevator. Press the button and it will take you directly to the 14th floor. Over there, a steward will remove your clothes and prepare you for the spa."

"Alright."

I go in, press the button, and count 20 seconds until the arrival. The door opens. A naked young man approaches. He's bearded, long-haired, and hairy all over his muscular body. He sports a metallic cock ring and greets me with a bow.

"This way, sir."

I follow him without taking my eyes off his powerfully built butt. This guy must have been in a football team. Or rugby. My erection pushes through the front fly of my boxers and tents in my trousers. He notices and smiles.

"That will be properly taken care of, don't worry, sir."

We finally get to a back walking closet, where I strip and James, that's his name, hangs my clothes neatly, and places them in a plastic bag with a name tag. For a minute, I watch my reflection on the mirror. My hair is falling. The entrances on my forehead are bigger every year. I'm not that old, though. I'm barely 26.

"Everything alright?" James asks.

"Yes. It's all good."

"Follow me, then."

James calls Nuke, a black guy whose sex almost reaches his left knee.

"Take good care of him. We want him to come back," James says. He winks at me, takes a small bow, and leaves.

"Lie down, sir," says Nuke.

I climb on the massage bed, and he immediately pours oil on my back, butt, and legs.

"Urgh, oil," I whine.

"Don't you like it?" he asks, genuinely invested in my comfort.

"Whatevs."

He caresses my flesh in circles, embracing the microscopic fibers in my skin, bit by bit approaching my anus with a skill that involves half an hour of fingering without fingering, tapping, pressing his palms against my hole, but never entering. At some point he reaches under me and pulls my dick back. He sucks it while still manipulating my legs. Then, he finally goes for my anus. I started leaking the park guy's cum and he just licks it clean.

"Someone fucked you before?" he asks.

"Yup. On my way here. Some guy in East Gordon Park."

"Gotta be careful with those guys. They ain't clean, if you know what I mean."

"So, what? Are you going to clean me now?"

"You want me to?"

"Just fuck me already. I want it."

"How much do you want it?"

"I'm dying for it."

He rams himself inside my ass without asking any more questions. By ramming, I mean his dick is like a battering ram, except battering rams are only meant to bring doors and gates down, and this one pierces. On these occasions, silence is a voyeur old friend.

However, the feeling of Nuke's oiled pubes brushing my crack send the vomit spiraling out.

"I'm sorry," I whimper. "I don't like hair. I'll clean it up. Bring me a mop and I'll do it."

"It's ok, sir. Don't worry about it," he says, visibly shaken. His erection falters and shrinks to the size of a stub. He's a grower, no doubt about it. Problem with growers is we can't hide our shame.

"I'm really sorry," I say, and leave.

While I trace my way to the showers, I wonder why I can't give up my disgust towards hair. There's this long-haired yogi type being double fucked on a bench by two bears. The sight repulses me. I take a shower as quickly as I can and leave for the lockers. James is there.

"Sir, are you ok? They told me you have had an *incident*." He stresses the word in a very slight way, almost to the point of a whisper. I am glad for it.

"Yeah. I'm really sorry. I'm a bit squeamish about hair. I'll clean it up if you bring me a mop."

"That's our job, sir. It's really no problem."

His erection is gone, though. Not him too.

As I put on my clothes, a hand puts a handkerchief on my nose and mouth and holds me tight with the other one. I lose consciousness almost immediately. All I remember are the dim lights and the many strong arms.

4.

When I open my eyes, James is lovingly kissing my legs and licking my feet.

"Please, don't do that."

"Wow. You're squeamish about so many things…"

"I can't help it. Why am I tied?"

"We'll kill your squeamishness, sir. It's part of our job."

"Oh, please, don't. I didn't mean any disrespect."

"You didn't disrespect us. This isn't about respect. In fact, this isn't about you. It's just policy. Now, chill."

I lie there, tied with black leather belts. Even my neck is tied, comfortably, but still held in place. I hear many steps.

"Is this the guy?" someone asks.

"Yup. He's the one who threw up at Nuke."

The man comes into view. It's the yogi who was double penetrated by the two bears.

"My name is Marco. I'll be your torturer today."

"Torturer?"

"Be quiet, sir. I'm just trying to do my job."

He climbs on the bed I am tied to, and just stands there, as if waiting for something. When I see the yellow stream leave his cock and splash on my face I try to cry, but he places his foot in my mouth and advises me not to scream or bite him. When he's done, he put his cock in between my lips.

"Slurp it clean. Come on. You're not as clean as you think. It doesn't matter how much you shave your body, or much antibacterial shit you put on your skin. You're just as dirty as the rest of us mortals."

The other men laugh. Some come closer and piss on my face and body. There's this brown guy who takes about five minutes emptying his bladder all over me. My mouth is forced open by several fingers.

"Drink, mutherfucker!"

I have to. The choice has been taken from me. There's something really bitter about the taste of it. If I had to imagine how defeat tastes, this would be it. Acrid. The way I always imagine the color ochre would taste. When the brown guy finishes, Marco squats on my face and bears down. I see his sphincter open and a white-red river splashes against my eyes, nose, and lips. Then, he shits. My mouth still pried open, I am forced to taste it, which, strangely enough, is sweet in the way 89% cocoa dark chocolate is sweet.

"Eat it. Swallow it."

Again, I throw up but this time no one cleans after me.

5.

As the minutes pass like hours, I am fucked and bred several times, used as toilet, force-fed feces, and used as bukkake victim. After several hours, I am taken to the showers, cleaned, leashed, and made to crawl like a dog with a canine rubber tail up my ass. I surprise myself at how easy it is to obey once the options, choices, and wishes are removed for me. My knees don't hurt as I crawl my way to the dirty dungeon, where several men await.

Some faces I do recognize. Others I don't. The CEO of the company is there, along with several of his aides. The manager of my department is there too, along with the accountant, who sits on the former's tiny, though extra thick cock. The CEO is busy eating shit off a twink's ass. As the young man poops, the old man chews and swallows. It amazes me just how easy it is to accept certain things once you see a room full of people doing and enjoying them. James sits on Nuke's cock, who sits on another guy's even bigger and shittier cock. Everyone pisses on each other and drinks piss. The scat feeding is communal. And suddenly, the most outrageous thought comes to me: this must be what communism looks like, even if people are too politically correct to admit it: everyone happily lapping up each other's feces.

The guy leading me claps loud and everyone stops what they're doing. I am red because of the attention, rather than the stink.

"I think he's ready, sir."

"Good," the CEO responds. "Bring him here."

I am led to the man's lap, where I climb and rest my butt.

"What a nice ass. It must be brimming full of shit. Take a poop for me."

I bear down and almost immediately, a huge snake leaves my innards. He catches it in his hands and brings it first to his nose, then to his mouth. He eats contentedly. Then, he smears the sides of my mouth with it. There's a technique here. He knows that everyone responds well to tenderness. He kisses my forehead with his smeared lips, and I open my mouth and eat my own shit. His hands are soft, like a pianist's.

"That's a good boy. You'll get far in this company."

"Thanks, sir," I say, as if a strange unspoken force compels me to say it. He smiles and gives me a full kiss on the mouth, his tongue prying my dirty lips open. Then, he squats on my face and shits. And of course, I eat.

Afterwards, everyone takes turns fucking me, breeding me, pissing on me, or shitting my face. Until only James remains.

"Now, let's deal with that aversion to hair."

6.

James takes me to the showers. This time, he's so lenient and loving. He lathers me with the most expensive body shampoo they have, the ones that are so expensive you only see them in boutiques or as part of some limited-edition bath works from brands that have naught to do with bath stuff, like lingerie or male underwear brands. He cleans himself too, his raging hard-on brushing my ass from time to time.

"You are beautiful. Whatever traumas you had in your childhood, it's time to let them go."

"How did you know…?"

"It's obvious, sir. An aversion to hair? That's as rare as it comes. I imagine it was a childhood thing. Wanna talk about it?"

"Not really, no."

"Well, you've already tasted and swallowed piss and shit. Bodily hair won't represent any trouble, I think, yes?"

I don't respond. Hair has that quality that makes everything look elastic, molten, dirty.

"Well, you're clean now. Wanna grab something to eat?"

"Yes. Thanks."

He takes me to a cafeteria at the end of the reception. The bear couple that fucked the yogi are heartily eating chicken noodle soup with vegetables and ham. It looks delicious. Another guy is having a veggie burger, and another is simply eating yogurt. Everyone looks comfortable enough and that appeases me.

"What do you wanna eat?" James asks.

"Cake. I'd like some cake."

The Jesus Man

This story is not about Jesus. I mean, it's not about the man who asked Simon Peter "Simon, son of John, do you love me more than these?" Certainly, not about the guy to cast the merchants out of the tabernacle or the guy who called out pharisees as "brood of vipers." This story is about another Jesús, an immigrant, born in Mexico.

I meet him on December 17, 2018, in his native Colima, as part of a series of articles I've been writing over the years, debunking miracle workers and faith healers all over the Americas. And this guy... I had received the most absurd accounts from witnesses all over the world. Stories about all types of miraclestuff, as they call his "works." I heard 13 accounts of him levitating, three reports of him being able to incept ideas telepathically, for instance, to cure addiction; five accounts of objects flying or floating around him, 16 people saw him transmute materials, and finally, 189 testimonials of people he healed, including, and this really upsets me I confess... amputees. And that is not even the weirdest thing that they say about him.

So, I pay him a visit with Jeremy, my assistant. We travel all the way to

Guadalajara, and from there, we pay the fare to Colima. When we get into town, the driver tells us that it is one of the smallest in Mexico.

"People here literally know each other," he says, but I know every single person in this planet who lives in a small town says the same thing.

"We are looking for the residence of the healer everyone's talking about."

"Jesús"? he asks and makes the sign of the cross.

"Yes. Why?"

He falls silent and pretends to listen to a song on the radio, even though the radio is off. Jeremy and I look at each other.

"This is the place," the driver finally says and drops us off in front of one of those neo-Colonial styled houses that are so common in countries and territories that were conquered and colonized by the Spaniards. The houses around it seem battered, like the world financial crisis touched them and laid them bare first, before the rest of the world. His house, however, looks more like a museum: conserved, preserved, like entropy has no dominion or right over it. It is painted teal, with no visible cracks, weeds, or dust. As if the house itself were alive and refusing to behave any other way than its very best. A very tall, white, lanky, and bearded hippie with blue eyes ("they're green," says Jeremy, "and he is black, what are you talking about?") comes to greets us at the car.

"*Hola.* Nice to meet you. My name is Jesús."

"Nice to meet you, Jesús. My name is Michael Fitz. I'm a journalist from The Associated Press. And this here is my assistant, Jeremy Miller."

"*Hola. Mucho gusto,*" he says, shaking our hands.

"So, Jesús, I'd like to interview you. Is it ok by you?"

He thinks about it for a while.

"Only without cameras," he responds.

"But we'd like to document your 'miraclestuff' and we can't do that if we don't tape this."

"Ok. You'll see what happens, then. How you deal with it is up to you."

He shows us his humble house, one floor, one bedroom, a bathroom that is more like a cupboard, joint kitchen and dining room, and walls that are laid bare. Not even a photograph of his family.

"Sit here," he says, as he pulls up three cheap collapsible chairs. After we do, he breaks the ice with a simple "So?" Everything about this guy is simple, inexpensive, and humble, yet clean, strong, and beautiful.

"Right," I answer. "I'm gonna set the equipment here, and the camera... here, and let's check the sound... testing, one, two, one two."

Both Jeremy and I see Jesús through the camera, but none of us notices anything strange.

"Alright. I think we're ready to go. First question: can you show us a small miracle?"

Jesús opens his palms and they are empty. He closes them in a prayer gesture and opens them again to reveal bleeding stigmata.

"Fucking hell!" Jeremy exclaims.

"I'm sorry. People are always startled."

"How...?" is the only question that escapes my mouth, and it comes out incomplete.

"How what? How do I do stuff? I don't know, man."

"Can you levitate?"

Jesús crosses his legs and sits like an Indian. Right in front of the camera, he hovers several feet above the ground, and gently comes back down.

"Whoa. That's... amazing!"

Jesús starts telling his story: he grows up here, in this village. When he turns 14, both of his parents die in a car accident. Jesús says he felt them pass away all the way from his room. And that's when, he says, it all starts. One day, while still mourning the loss of his parents, a single tear drops from his right eye and falls on a dry and withered patch of grass. Not only does the yellowed and dead grass become alive and green again, but the land in the entire town goes verdant again and full to the brim with flowers. All over town, people fall to their knees praising God for this miracle, but then, they get up, and follow the trail of green and rainbow petals to its source: a battered Jesús crying his guts out for his parents. Unleashed grief turned unbridled force of creation.

No one offers to soothe Jesús, or even words of comfort. Instead, people charge toward him in an instinctive attempt to touch or grab some part of this angel who has been sent from Heaven to bring back the spring, fending back the cold that comes from the dormant Colima volcano. Someone grabs his T-shirt, another touches his hair, and all of a sudden, everyone touches a part of him, and the release of the healing wave leaves him overstimulated, convulsing on the floor, as if possessed, and visibly erect, as if the electricity in his entire body had gone awry.

Then, a neighbor stands up to the crowd.

"Everyone, I need a circle. He needs air. Back off, *cabrones*!"

He steps in and takes Jesús inside his house.

"I'll take care of you whenever I can, Jesús," he says. "You don't owe them anything."

The neighbor steps out and addresses the crowd.

"You all better keep your mouths shut."

They nod and seem to agree. And naturally, next day, people from all over Mexico are already camping in a tent city erected during the night and the wee hours. They have heard the story, the message, the news, and the memes of the one who made the town green and made the flowers grow.

Carlos, Jesús's rescuer the night before, is so livid that the veins over his temples tremble.

"The Apostle is furious," some people start saying already.

"What in the actual fuck?" mutters Carlos.

Jesús steps in and addresses those in attendance.

"My friends, I am but a kid. I cannot help you all. I don't even know what I am or how I did what I did yesterday."

But they don't leave. They want to witness.

"He's a white angel," one old lady among the crowd says.

"What? He ain't white," says a man nearby. "Can't you see his eyes? They're Asian."

"What?" asks Carlos, who has always seen him as a beach-bleached mulatto.

Jesús interrupts them with a finger to his lips, walks among them, and touches several people. Immediately, amputees regrow their lost limbs, those on wheelchairs stand up again, and those with crutches are able to discard them. He heals a woman riddled with aids. Her Kaposi sarcoma stains disappear right in front of everyone's eyes. And they stay in their tents.

"You know, again, I'm a kid and I need my privacy. You all said you would leave after I healed you."

But they don't leave. Instead, more people arrive from all over Mexico, and this time, from other parts of the Americas, like this guy from a Kalaallit tribe in Greenland, who is a healer himself and wants to learn from a master.

"I'm not a master, man. You probably know more than I do," Jesús says, but also, he lights the tip of his finger with fairy lights and touches the Kalaallit man's forehead, and suddenly, the man's eyes go really white, and come back to their natural black.

"All those formulas... all those plant combinations... all those recipes... I could heal my entire country with this knowledge!" Then, he falls on his knees and starts crying in gratitude, and Jesús, who is still fourteen and mourning his own parents, starts crying too, and all of a sudden, the whole town is crying, and that day becomes known as the *Día de Lágrimas*, celebrated every year as the day Colima gets its own Messiah.

After that... well, the people never leave. They become his neighbors and help finish raising him. If it takes an entire village to raise a normal kid, it takes an entire city to raise a child of God.

When Jesús hits the majority of age, he tells Carlos, his neighbor turned big brother turned guardian, that he wants to see the world.

"I knew this day was coming," he says and starts crying. "Go on, then, little bro. But, please come back."

So, in a sort of compromise, Jesús promises to go back and forth between wherever he decided to go and his beautiful Colima. That way, he can always come back to take care of his people. And that is his story up to now.

Jeremy and I immediately turn to our videos of Jesús. When I am the one doing the recording, he is white, long-haired, and blue-eyed. The classic depiction of Jesus Christ. But when Jeremy is the one behind the camera, Jesús looks like a mixed-race bodybuilder.

"What the what?"

"Yeah. I discovered it too soon."

"So... is it always like that? Do you always look different when different people see you?"

"So it would seem."

"And what about what you look like to you?"

"I haven't looked in a mirror since I discovered this. It's traumatic."

"But you must have seen yourself before that, right?"

"Yes. But really, I no longer remember how I really look."

There is some silence, after which he asks "Do you have all you needed for your interview?"

"Yes, thank you, Jesús."

"Thank you. After all, it was nice to tell my story, Mr. Fitz."

"Call me Michael, please."

"Thank you, Michael. So, aside from your journalistic duty, have you and Jeremy come to be healed?"

Jeremy and I look at each other.

"Healed from what?"

He looks at us sadly.

"Jeremy has a brain tumor, and you have the beginnings of Type-2 diabetes."

We look at each other with quizzical looks. How the fuck did he know?

<<I'm also a telepath, among other things,>> he incepts directly into their minds. <<So, do you want to be healed or not?>>

An Embrace from a Beautiful Stranger Who Drowned Forever

I.

Just as he enters the murky, challenging waters of La Pared Beach, he knows one of them will be lost. He's a single lifeguard, after all, a single as in only one for the entire beach. He can't save them both. As he swims against the currents, the sea swallowing and vomiting him at times, casting him in and out of the froth, he grabs his husband's hand, then the forearm, and pulls. But the sea has another idea.

"Esteban!"

But his husband is lost in the deep. His black-haired, red-bearded husband. The most beautiful man in the world. Now the most beautiful drowned.

Back at the beach, the relatives await. The people who have attended their wedding wait. Expect. Demand. All faces search in Alberto's face for a clue, a sign of life, that Esteban is not lost to the sea, that their worst collective nightmare has not transpired in an unforeseen instant, that their beloved suicide has not, in fact, achieved his goal in the most beautiful of days.

Esteban was Alberto's first man ever. Has been. Is. Time loses meaning in the sea, and the beach is just a threadbare extension, a mercy of connection to a solid place in life. Time means nothing even in an interim of ten years married to a woman he no longer could erect himself for, and who soon becomes his best friend. A fag hag. A time hag.

Alberto meets Esteban through Marie herself. Marie, beautiful, unbridled flamehead Marie. Fiery dog trainer and cat psychologist Marie. They have agreed to live together in the same house. It's the dogs and the cats who catch the whiff first. Not a one of the huskies and calicos dares go near Esteban. As if they know not to form attachments.

One day, Esteban proposes. Alberto says yes. Marie even takes the celebrant courses and gets her license. She will officiate. She did. Has done. Does. They set the day, get the permits to use the beach, rent their black tuxes, and off they go to their fate. Or their doom. The difference is silly. A hair. A millimeter. A failed farewell.

Esteban's family knows. His arms and legs are covered in Xs cut with knifes, presumably by himself. Father, Mother, and Brother discover them the day they see the nurse take Esteban's clothes off in order to dress him with that sterile and boring hospital robe. The insides of the thighs even have question marks carved into the flesh, like African tattoos in some tribes, a relief of skin hardened by time in its merciless punishment. They look at each other and certify their beliefs in a communion of eyes and sighs.

"I hope he gets to be happy," Mother says. "I want him to have that, at least."

"He will," replies Father in a foolish attempt at consolation.

After the ceremony, Esteban tells Alberto.

"I wanna go for a swim. Wanna come, dear?"

"Not today, *papi*. The currents are all crazy. It's too dangerous."

"All the more reason, scaredy-cat. That's life for you. Look at it."

The froth or foam or Triton Sea King's cum parts the ocean in weird, intrinsic patterns. The sea is not supposed to behave like that. Not unless you are in a beach that was never meant to be a beach but is made a bitch by human hands. This place had been claimed by mankind several centuries ago, when the Spaniards refilled it with a layer of rock and several others of sand. Time, again, has made it a place of death, where people come for the ultimate thrill, a risk of no return.

"You shouldn't go, either. It's our wedding. We should be drinking, dancing, having fun…"

"Oh, don't be a sourpuss. It'll all be alright. I'll be back in a jiff."

"Esteban, please be careful."

"I will."

And yet, Alberto can't trust him enough. As Esteban removes his tux and underwear, and steps into the waters naked, Alberto knows, just as his in-laws have known. It's all a matter of nudity. Of delivering yourself to death just as life has delivered you. He follows his lover with his sight, just like everyone else does. And then, he's gone. A change of froth. Or foam. Or Triton Sea King's cum. He's swallowed. Alberto doesn't bother to remove his clothes. Off he goes after the suicidal love of his life.

II.

Helicopters overfly the area for days. Several boats join the search. But contrary to popular opinion, the sea keeps whatever it takes. On the sixth day, the search is suspended. The coronel concludes that Esteban has been lost. He is declared dead. Has been. Is.

"What are you gonna do now, Al?" Marie asks.

"Keep the house. I'm leaving."

"Wait. Why?"
"I can't stay here."
"Why?"
"Because I feel like joining him."

And thus, Alberto moves to Florida, where every Puerto Rican eventually ends up.

III.

"Hello. What can I do for you?" the woman behind the counter asks.

"Hi. I'm here for the interview with Mr. Coleman," Al responds.

"Sure. Let me check. Oh, here it is. You are punctual. Mr. Coleman will see you in ten."

"Thanks."

He looks around the office. The position is as an independent consultant for a firm that builds water parks, and which specializes in wave makers. The pay is too good.

Mr. Coleman appears and beckons him to enter. He turns out to be a Cornish refugee who made his life building pools in the least respectful state of the Union. That much Alberto is able to surmise according to his surroundings at the man's office. Several pictures on the wall: him poking his head through the hole of one of the stones of the Mên-an-Tol, him standing alone besides the Mên Scryfa, him besides the bee sculpture in the Eden Project...

"Do you like what you see?" Coleman inquires.

"Sure, I mean, that's Cornwall, right?"

"Did the accent betray me or was it the pictures?"

"Both."

"Have you been to my homeland, my lad?"

"Only in dreams."

The man smiles. What definitely used to be pearly whites is now clouded by layers of what could only be considered life. He opens a drawer and takes out a pipe with some tobacco of unrecognizable scent, pours some in, lights it, and smokes while longingly looking at the pictures. Longingly as in looking through them. Pupils momentarily dilated.

"I dream of returning someday."

"What made you leave, sir?"

"Sir, huh? Points in your favour. Well, I was disowned by my family in a time when being disowned was the worst possible punishment your kin could inflict on you. It was the 60s. Parents often disowned their children if they suspected they were communists. It was what they did to maintain appearances of loyalty to the Crown."

Alberto takes in the size of this stranger, his puffing and powerful chest, yet constricted in that slim-fitted white shirt and black tie. His hair and beard are white, and he sports one of those hipster revival looped mustaches, yet it looks the real deal in him. He wears black suspenders that perfectly match his Oxfords. His white V-neck undershirt could not cover the ink of his arms and beginnings of chest, colorful ink in bright hues. Al surprises himself being erect.

"Are you or were you a communist?"

"I wouldn't know. See, lad, to be a communist you have to live in communism. There has never been such a thing."

"Not even in Cuba or the U.S.S.R.?"

"Those were dreams of communism that never took real root. Cuba, for instance, is state capitalism. True communism is impossible in this world."

He inhales a big amount of smoke, and then offers me some. I think of refusing but decide against. Instead, I inhale a bit. It tastes of blood and strawberries. And carrion pie.

"It's an acquired taste, I know," he says, after seeing my face.

"It's putrid."

"Yes, but it's also good for the soul. So... to the task at hand. I've studied your resume, verified your references, education, and work history. I'm ready to give you a chance."

"Thanks, sir."

"You may call me Melv."

"As in Melvin?"

"No. Just Melv."

IV.

From the tender age of 12, Alberto has known that Father Sea is a capricious creature. He may take, retake, keep, or vomit anything He wishes. That July 13, 1980, the Ole Man takes a young woman. She is surfing and a sudden rogue wave tosses her into the air. Upon hitting the water, she loses consciousness and drowns. Alberto is alone on the beach. He and his friends used to skinny deep there, especially after school or upon skipping class. They would cast off their earthly attachments in the form of clothes and leave them in a neat pile on the black and white sand, a black and white crushed like Oreos for a pie crust, a neat pile like an offering to forbidden gods.

That day, though, Alberto is alone, his skyclad form bathed in the soft sunlight that comes from such a tropical and indecisive climate. One minute the sun shines, the next a dark cumulonimbus threatens to drown the world in a biblical deluge. And by God, how Alberto hates indecision, whether in weather or in people.

The woman doesn't even scream. Alberto wants to close his eyes. He doesn't know how to swim. The woman floats for a while and then slips down, like a paper boat origami. That woman is a paper doll when the paper can no longer hold or soak any more water and loses the fight against the immensity of such a liquid sea. Alberto wants to close his eyes. There is naught he can do, after all. But Father Sea has other plans. The Old God makes the kid watch.

V.

Being an independent consultant for a wave maker builder means a lot of work with no office of his own. This means that Alberto will be walking around all day, measuring places for future or possible pools. It means doing the work alone. He quickly gets used to it, and people usually leave him alone, already used to the man wearing tank tops and shorts.

Melv Coleman takes his example and starts coming to office in a more relaxed attire. He is happy those days, old Melv. He even buys a small fridge and equips it with some booze and makes a sort of desk in his office for Alberto. They will take long walks together, surveying possible clientele and spaces, and come back to a light beer with their lunch. They laugh a lot. Melv is a good joker; he has been collecting these jokes from all around the world. But Alberto has a darker humor and a biting wit to boot. They will make entire joke tournaments until the dark.

One night, as Melv is about to leave, Alberto blocks his path with a raised leg. As they look at each other, they know.

"I had been waiting for this moment since I interviewed you," Melv comments as a very exhausted Alberto adjusts his head on Melv's furry chest.

"Me too," the young man answers.

"I'd like to know you better."

Alberto passes out listening to the silver fox's heart.

VI.

The launching party of the Belmont Adventure Water Park is on June 17, 2003. All kinds of local celebrities —which in this town meant the sheriff and his wife, the weather lady, the librarian, two upbeat and three serious writers and the local judge— appear, along with families and their kids. The press covers the news all day, as there's apparently nothing better to do that day in the town of Belmont.

Melv and Alberto interact with the people but pay close attention to what is to become the "main event": the Talula Wave

Rider, a 2.5 square mile of water with fake lotus leaves and plastic logs floating on it. At 6:00 p.m. the bell tolls, and the park goers launch themselves into a frenzy in order to get to the water. The waves start at 6:15 p.m. after a brief speech from the builders. People clap as people casually do in these cases. When the first wave hits, Alberto knows something must be off. It isn't a wave, but more like a tsunami. Children scream and parents tell them to calm down and laugh nervously while looking around at other adults who do the same.

"There's something wrong with the generators, Al."

"I'm on it."

The third wave comes and washes away half of the pool population, who take it upon themselves to run back to the water, all the while laughing and screaming in bliss. The fourth wave washes them back even further from the beach. The fifth one goes almost unnoticed, rocks forth and then back again to join with the sixth wave, which indeed, becomes a tsunami.

"It's out of control!"

"Turn it off!"

"Already did! But look!"

Most of the people are able to duck and swim under the giant wave, except for a guy in his headphones. A white skinny guy in his thirties, who looks like Clark Gable with curly hair. The wave hits him hard and tosses him several yards into the cement, and drags him back to the water fold, drowning him instantly. By the time Al gets to him, he has a dead man in his arms. He carries the victim to the shore and gives him CPR, but to no avail. The press covers the news. Calls it a freak accident. Freak is the right word to describe such incidents, but not on media. Never on media. The park closes after its maiden voyage. A week later, Alberto steps on a plane back to Puerto Rico. His country, and the land of his beauiful suicide.

VII.

One day, he sees what, at first, he thinks is a speck of dust on his left eye. He looks at the sea beyond La Pared. It's a person floating on the water. He immediately swims the hardly known ocean current trail, hardly known as currents there change every day. But he knows how to feel and circumvent Father Sea's whims. He dashes here and zigzags there, until he is about to reach the person. For a minute, he just stands there, floating, the face of his husband Esteban regarding the sky like a lover lost in centuries of dealings with false gods. As he approaches the figure, the Sea swallows him again. After all, the Sea keeps everything it takes.

How to Turn into a Faeling

I meet Darren the first day of Spring 99'. We bump into each other as he comes out of the only available cubicle in the library bathroom. A burst of electricity nearly burns my elbow skin.

"Sorry. Static," he says and smiles.

"There's no static in the tropics," I reply without knowing why.

He smiles again and makes for the exit without washing his hands.

I don't see him again for a couple of days, but everyone talks about him in the faculty. Everyone has something to say about the tall white stranger with the aquiline nose, who went from smooth face to full beard in one day. Charlie says he's an ex-Marine, former merc from Afghanistan. Darla corrects him. It was never Afghanistan but Iraq. Nobody agrees, however, on the colour of his eyes. Jenny swears they're blue and that he's originally from Canada. Jorge remarks that his eyes are green and that they remind him of his backyard in Cidra, what with all the mango trees, the heliconias, and the giant ferns. The day we bump into each other, I swear I see yellow eyes. Like those of a cat.

I meet him again one night at Eros, our community's favourite club. I am dancing with a friend, or more like moving. I don't dance. Not really. It's almost midnight and the club fills to brim with dancers, protohipsters, coke sniffers, and some Spaniards from the student exchange program. A go-go boy appears in full Pocahontas regalia minus the dress, plus the feathers and war paint. He takes off his tiny golden thong to reveal a 13-inch spear, which he earnestly caresses until he turns, bends over, and opens his cheeks to offer a panoramic view of his rock-solid ass. His body seems robbed from one of those sculpture ateliers that people oft see in ancient European cities like Florence and Luxemburg. Even the ring of his hole has that stone hewn quality. He sucks a finger, inserts it into his bum, and the crowd goes wild... with the new "Thriller" remix, for nobody except I is really paying attention to him. So, he focuses on me and his cum hits me in the eye.

"Fuck! It hurts!"

"Are you ok, buddy?"

When I turn, there he is, a napkin in hand. He carefully wipes the go-go boy's cum off my eyes, glasses, and chin.

"I'm afraid it's gonna hurt for a while."

"I'm used to hurt."

"I can see that," he says, though I don't know why.

When I regain my sight all I can see is a tall bloke, the size of a tower, a giant golem of shining metal. He must be 6'6" or close. And he... shines. Some sort of light hits him from behind, or he must have sprayed some party glow paint on his skin. But he glows.

"Did you come alone?"

"Like I always do."

"Wanna dance?"

"Right. Dancing. Are you sure you have what it takes to move this crane?"

He laughs, grabs my waist with his powerful hands, and forces me to move. We are dancing to some stupid Nina Flowers remix, but I get into it and feel myself arrive to the point where I no longer care about stupid. He braves the small distance between our bodies and grabs my ass.

"I want you, little buddy."

"Yeah, take me to your place, please."

We laugh and make for the exit.

"Where do you live?" I ask once we're out in the street.

"Close enough. We can walk."

And so, we walk for two or three minutes until we arrive at 457 Malén St., which is besides an old armoury. He opens the rusty gate of the olive green with bright blue brimmed house, and all I can see is a most beautiful garden with plants whose green glows at 2:30 in the wee hours.

"How…?"
"It's the drugs, buddy."
Inside the house, we kiss ardently.
"So, you liked the go-go boy?"
"Uhm, sure."
"Well, you're sure gonna love mine."
And he strips to reveal a veiny, pulsating 16-inch wyrm that hooks up to his owner's face.
"I'm not sure what we can do with that," I sentence.
"It'll be like walking on a cloud, I assure you."

He smiles and again I see that glow in his skin. I go on fours and brace myself. But all I remember is being filled little by little, as if his cock had gone into me in a flaccid state and had quietly grown once inside. And then, silk.

"Your ass is so warm. Wow."

I can't speak. He slowly fills me. I can feel him reaching some ultimate sphincter I can't name now, and when he achieves it, I feel strong golem hands grab hold of my chest under my arms and immobilize me.

"You're mine now."

And then he fucks me. A horse cock. A bull. A dragon. Somehow, I feel like bubble gum that is stretched as far as it can go without breaking. I feel thin. I am bubble gum and he is chewing me and could spit me out any minute.

"Do you like it?"

But I can't speak. My body takes over and my ass moves of its own accord. I twerk like a lowlife.

"If you keep doing that, you're gonna make me cum."

And he cums in torrents of light. His starglow invades me, makes me full, his rays of sun blind me. He is a blue gas giant, hot and all-encompassing, almighty, and full of gravity. I am a miserable moon attached to his orbit. He's right. I am his.

"Shit. What a hot ass, *papi*."

When I open my eyes, the world has changed. Gardens hang all around us. Soft twilights reveal deep and bright greenery with blue, turquoise, and purple wisterias, white oleanders, and fragrant hyacinths.

"Where are we?"

"You're in Fae. My home. You kinda knew."

"Sort of."

"Well, you're here, you're queer. I love you. Please, stay. Even for a while. Just stay a bit."

And he embraces me again.

"Wait. I have so many questions."

"Like?"

"You read at my university. You live in my city. Yet you are a... I'm sorry, what are you?"

"I'm a Faeling."

"A what?"

"Fae-ling. The male of the fairy."

"How come you don't have wings?" I ask, not really knowing why. Stupid question, honestly.

"Wanna see them?"

And he opens his wings, wild gossamer things, like those of a dragonfly, but full of stars and sparkles of no discernible colour. Grand two-meter things, round at the edges, soft, and ethereal. His own light is refracted through them, and all I see is a thousand pieces of rainbow. Like Skittles.

"They are beautiful."

"Would you like a pair?"

And then, he fucks me again and again empties inside me. I feel my skin start to glow every time he breeds me.

"Will I become like you?"

"Only if you want to."

The English Teacher

The day Mr. Lovelace arrives at our slums, the kids are so happy they come out of their makeshift cardboard and stick-walled huts. Some parents come out too of their homes, mostly to inspect the tall, ginger, bearded white man. Over the years, they have learned to distrust white people, particularly Americans, as most of these villagers have been displaced by the growing bed-and-breakfast industry in Thailand. Most of these children are orphans, and part of the Peace Corps English teacher job description is to care for those orphans, to give them love, instruction, and feed them. He will receive a generous yet special stipend from the organization to do so.

"Hi," he says in perfect Thai to one of the adults, and then to the kids. "I'm Jeffrey Lovelace, the new teacher. Nice to meet y'all."

I watch as my people go out of their way to welcome this stranger and make him feel at home. I hardly have the energy to pretend I care about him. I'd rather run naked on the nearest beach, which features a sort of mountains that are, in reality, stone claws or fingers covered in greenery that rise up from the very sea, quite close to the beach. You can swim there and will reach it in 5 maybe 10 minutes. I go to the nearest all the time, and I have named it *Niw khxng thale* or The Fingers of the Sea. Last time I climbed that particular finger, I sat on the top and emptied my mind in the wind, the seagulls, and finally, the stars against the purple-blue-green night.

They take Mr. Lovelace to what will be his hut and classroom. Most of the orphan kids sleep there in a makeshift room with several bunk beds. That's where I sleep. The hut has no bathroom, and thus, no shower. He seems unfazed by this and doesn't even react when we tell him that we usually bathe in the beach and shit in the forest. "*Tking,*" he says to everyone and everything. "Ok."

Finally, he says: "First lesson starts now," and everyone, both kids and adults, sit up and take notice. "I need help making improvements to the village's structures. It's hard work, but I'm from Arkansas, and I was a builder before I became a teacher."

So, the next few weeks, Mr. Lovelace mixes his tasks with instruction for the kids and the adults. "Why do we plaster the walls?" he'd ask. "So we don't get wind inside our homes. Or critters," the kids would respond. "And why do you make sure to make the roofs waterproof?" he would inquire. "To protect us against the rain," we'd answer. And so on, so forth. "I can't feed you all the time," he'd often say, "but I can teach you to fish, hunt, and work what little land you have, so you can feed yourselves." This was his first lesson to us: *learn to fish by yourself, and when you master it, teach others as well.*

Those first days, he would tag along the villagers whenever they went to shit in the forest or bathe in the sea. It was important for him to show that he was one of us. The first time I see him drop his pants and squat close to some trees, I spy him from behind. His ass is like two huge mountains that hide a round, pink, and hairy crevasse —I've loved that word ever since he taught it to me—, and I have never seen people be so white back there. Everything in him is so pink and red, even the hair on his cock and armpits. He is like a God to me, hair like sun fire, skin like daylight, eyes like the sea. And when he bathes in the beach, he looks like a merman, like someone who actually came from the very sea to wash away his dirt, when nothing actually gets dirty in the deep. Sometimes, he comes out erect, but no one says anything because it often happens to the village men too.

The first few months with Mr. Lovelace see the construction of clay houses that the Thailand sun would bake almost immediately, to better house the villagers.

The homes are small, and Mr. Lovelace would later confess that he integrated what he knew as a builder with stuff that he saw on videos (he spends an entire week explaining to us what a video is) on TikTok and Instagram (a whole month goes to explain what cellphones and apps are and how they work). It takes us all patience and a lot of hard work, but by the end of the year, not only do we have solid houses that can stand the test of typhoons and the monsoon season, but the government of the Province of Phuket, with the aid of the Peace Corps' subprogram that Mr. Lovelace belongs to, provides windmills for electricity, plumbing and sewage services.

"How do you want to name this place, Jeff?" one of the adult women of the village asks when the construction is all over and done.

"Don't you have a name for it?" he inquires. "Y'all must have thought of something." And they look at me. "Anurak? Any ideas?"

"*Niw khxng thale*," I respond immediately. "Fingers of the Sea, Phuket, Thailand," I sentence.

They approve immediately, and Mr. Lovelace's final manual labor is to fell a tree, carve several planks, nail them, and glue them together with an epoxy-like sap, to paint on it the name of the village in bold and brave phosphorus white.

"Your turn," he tells me. "Hammer it down," and he passes me the mallet.

For the next two years, we orphans live, eat, play with, and learn from Mr. Lovelace all sorts of things: English, Thai, American and British literature, science, math, architecture, music, dance, art, health, home economics... although Mr. Lovelace's specialty is English. It takes him three months, after the infrastructure of the village is solid enough, to bring electricity, computers, and Internet, and five months to teach us how to use it all. But soon thereafter, he changes the way he teaches, and starts using PowerPoint modules for everything.

"As long as you have modules, the topic doesn't matter. You'll master it in no time."

"There's a magic to PowerPoint," he says. "A magic to how technology helps people learn," he says.

"We are lucky to have Mr. Lovelace with us," one of the seniormost villagers pronounces.

"Indeed," says another.

They look at me, and I know what they mean.

That night, after Mr. Lovelace falls asleep on his bed, which is sort of separated from our bunk beds by mere feet, I get up, walk over, go in bed with him, and close my eyes. Still asleep, he notices my presence —in the way that people asleep can notice anything—, turns to face me, and pulls me into a spooning embrace. Feeling his crotch against my butt gives me a fever that I don't understand well. I cannot help myself and start rubbing against him. He goes erect and his breathing patterns change, so I stop for a while, until he's snoring lightly, almost imperceptibly, again. Then I resume my rubbing. He tightens his hold on me and returns the motion, then caresses my chest with his right hand, softly pinching my nipple under my T-shirt, then going lower to enter the space between my skin and the waistband of my slip, probing, looking for my sleeping mollusk. I lower my slip, he removes his daddy briefs, and by now I know he has woken up and we are both trying complicitly to be quiet, because we know we can't wake the others. He spits on his hand and lathers the space between my butt cheeks with his drool. Then, he enters me ever so slightly. And goes back to sleep and turns away.

I am left wondering what the hell just happened, but I am still erect, so this time I spit, lather him up back there, and push against his walls. He mutters something unintelligibly low, so, I keep going. I keep pushing my penis in. I know it goes deep, because the pubes of his base brush against my pelvis and it kinda itches. I scratch myself lightly and ride him, slowly at first so as not to make him cry in pain, and then harder, until he wakes up again, whimpers something in my ear that I can't really understand, and I spray inside. Then, he turns me and pushes himself inside me with a vengeance. I almost cry out, but resignation can sometimes give you a higher power. Soon thereafter, he ejaculates inside me and falls asleep again almost immediately, still inside me. I fall asleep in the arms of the White God from the Land Beyond the South China Sea.

He wakes me up in the wee hours, before the other orphans can open their eyes, and takes me to bathe in the sea. Then, we swim to my mountain-finger, climb to the top, and just stay there, watching the sunrise. "I'll say this and nothing more," he starts. "I like you." I don't reply. What's there to say to that?

We keep fucking almost every night for the next two years. We steal every moment we can to fuck each other brainless, whether during the rice harvest, or under the massive and famous 15-minute rains brought by the monsoon season, or while picking vegetables and fruit from the humongous hydroponic tower. The villagers know and do not care, or at least, no one has given me any indication of caring. As the years go by, the seniormost start dying. And we the orphans become the adults. At some point, Mr. Lovelace says "I have to go back to my country. I can't stay here any longer."

"Why?" I ask.

But he just sends me a link to my cellphone. It's a news article. Thousands of young people take to the streets making a three-finger salute, a resistance symbol, demanding democracy and peace, mainly in Bangkok, but quickly spreading like a virus among all the provinces. They demand a new constitution, and for the "Prime Minister Prayut [to] step down as a first step toward ending authoritarian rule, cronyism, corruption, and government inefficiency." The most violent demonstrations occur in the Din Daeng district. The protesters, referred to by the media as the *Taluh Gas* —mostly kids as young as 13, the age I was when Jeffrey first came to the village— vandalize and burn traffic booths, police patrol cars, and portraits of the monarchs and royals. The riot police division employ water cannons mixed with dyes and teargas components, along with rubber bullets against the crowds. Every picture in the article shows kids no older than the orphans and I, bloodied, with bruises and gashes in their arms, legs, and faces. Yet the kids fight back with rocks, slingshots, fireworks, and even Molotov cocktails.

"The Peace Corps have already called me," Jeffrey says. "They are evacuating everyone from the country. I have to leave."

"What about me?" I ask.

"Anurak, I love you unconditionally. But I can't take you with me."

"Why not?"

He cannot face me, so I start repeating the question over and over, as he tries to escape me by putting his clothes and very few possessions in his truck. "Why not? Why not? Why not?" I inquire frantically, until he slaps me. I start crying, hopelessly trying to tie the man I have come to love all these years with my tears. He embraces me.

"It's not like I want to leave. And it's not like I'll leave forever. I'll come back, I promise. But your place is here, Anurak. Keep the village growing. Make it stronger, healthier. Protect it."

He withdraws a little, looks at me with his stupid, and honestly, ridiculous White God face that I just adore, and plants a kiss in my lips. I let go in that kiss because I know it will be the last.

"I'll always love you," and with those words, he finishes his business in Thailand, steps on his truck, and as he drives away, lost into the forest, I seek refuge in the power of resignation.

The Unsolvable Problem

"It's not the water," says a scientist.

"It's not the air," says another one.

"Then, why do we see what we see?" we all wonder.

On September 25, 2024, everyone on the planet wakes up to screams all over the globe. People wake up to see patterns of strange little, medium-sized, and big holes with spider eyes. We see this everywhere we look. And it causes a global panic. The U.S. blames China, because, why not? After all, China was to blame when, in 2023, it was finally revealed that covid-19 had "broken out" of a Wuhan lab, like we all knew, but were forced to ignore by political correctness. And let's not even go into the whole Chinese balloon fiasco of earlier that same year.

Imagine waking up to Carlos, my husband, and the first thing I see is his otherwise chiseled and perfect face deplored by patterns of holes, at first like blackheads, but which broaden before your very eyes to become holes from which tiny eyes emerge. Those million little eyes defacing Carlos's lips, and nose, and even his ginger beard, gaze upon you, pass judgment, and find you lacking.

By week two, people can't stop vomiting, particularly when eating. It's not nice to eat spaghetti with holes on them. And covering your eyes doesn't work. As soon as you picture what you are eating in your mind, it comes with holes in it.

By week three, all my nerve fibers awaken uncontrollably, and the scratch reflex takes over. So, we all get used to letting our fingernails grow, like those of cats, and you can see people scratching each other on the streets, a kind of social grooming. There's an even stranger feeling: electric sparks all over my body that leave me in a kind of perpetual Tourette Syndrome state. Everywhere you go, you see people, animals, and buildings with holes in them, but you also see people scratching the hell out of themselves and making sudden electric movements. Only humans act this way. Animals seem unfazed.

You get used to anything after a while. We've had to. In four years, we've had two category 5 hurricanes, tornadoes, hail, and even earthquakes since January. People in Puerto Rico joke about this shit, saying that "all we're missing is aliens," because, well, my people are like that, resilient through harsh, self-immolating, colonized humor. But, for instance, having to stop a conference to scratch yourself, or scratch the emcee, or picture a mother having to bathe her newborn child despite her disgust, or the boy who fears his daddy because of the many little monsters on his face and arms, or picture your husband trying to fuck you from behind and all he can see is that goddamn pattern of waves and waves of tiny little holes, and there comes the itchiness and the sparks on the skin, and the uncontrollable fit of scratching, scratching, scratching, and he withdraws, flaccid, because my high-maintenance, gym chiseled back, from which a hard butt suddenly protrudes, looks like something dead, withered, and full of baby spiders, and who wants to fuck that? And why should I blame him, when all I feel is that I'm being fucked by a putrid zombie full of pimples and blackheads? And so, this is how we pass the seemingly endless days, the new normal days, the days that we're living in.

On the fourth week, we're contacted by astronaut, Dr. Henry Gallagher, PhD PsyD. We had completely forgotten about our people in space. In the middle of a call with Agent Pérez of Cape Canaveral, verifying the state of Damrung 10BX Space Station, he discovers the horrible antic that has taken hold of humanity down here in the Earth. It's definitely something here, because he and his fellow scientists and cosmonauts are more than safe and sound.

"It'd be interesting to know if leaving the planet solves the problem," Dr. Gallagher concludes.

So, a decision is made, and world leaders create a lottery: the selected few would go live on the satellite colony. Again, chaos ensues, as everyone wants to leave the globe. Two of the first selected are murdered and their lottery tickets stolen for nothing: the killers would not be able to use those tickets or risk incarceration. So the world governments meet again and devise a new form of lottery, one driven by a planetary face-recognition archive sweepstakes. I end up being selected to fly up there, to the Damrung 10BX Space Station. I accept, on condition that my husband Carlos is allowed to come with me.

Two days later, we're strapped to a rocket and launched. During the trip, the moment we exit the stratosphere, I stop seeing *it*. So does my husband. But that's not all. When we exit the stratosphere, I stop hearing a particular sound that I didn't know I was hearing until then, but I had been hearing something.

Two years later, they will finally identify the unsolvable problem: a telluric confrontation brings about a persistent stream of pressure that produces a global tinnitus effect. Unfortunately, the almost imperceptible sound affects the parts of the human brain dealing with balance, pattern recognition, and texture perception. And there's nothing that anyone can do, except finally leave the planet on a starship colony, or remain and wait it out for who knows how many decades.

"We're already here," Carlos says.

"Right. We are."

Plop!

I grab the *Condorito* magazine from the stand while we wait for the line at the supermarket.

"I'm not paying for that," Mother says.

"Why?" I ask.

"That's mundane stuff. Not proper for Jehovah's Witnesses, like us."

Like you, you mean, a rebellious voice sasses in my head, but I dare not say anything. Instead, I ignore the "DO NOT READ THE MAGAZINES!!!" sign and read it as quickly as I can, while Mother does the line.

Condorito, the character, is an anthropomorphic condor although he almost has no plumage at all, save for a small tail composed of three red feathers, and a small collar of two rows of three or four white feathers apiece surrounding his neck, which kinda looks like the collar of his T-shirt. He sports black slacks, the legs rolled up and the knees patched over due to normal wear and tear, and his iconic red sandals. His head is round and shaved, with a prominent beak under a pair of huge eyes, between which hangs a medium-sized, bean-shaped crest that also serves, conveniently, as a high brow.

Characterization is everything in this comic magazine, almost to the point of being rude, like Charlie Hebdo, so by dressing like this, the author, Chilean illustrator Pepo, wants us to understand Condorito's place in the world: kinda like a hillbilly, but savvy and representing the working class. The comic magazine is a Chilean force to be reckoned even against *MAD*. I remember loving just how much it could be done with only four colors: orange, cream, black, and green. And the humor gets me. It's a softened kind of ghoulish delight that, kept to a 30-page magazine every month, is more than enough.

The issue I'm reading while Mother approaches the line is a kind of anthology of the best strips in 40 years. In a single-page strip, Condorito is dressed like a waiter and is straining coffee using a colorful sock before a bewildered foodie. The strip reads *"Pruebe nuestro café de la casa: FILTRO ESPECIAL."* Try our homemade coffee: special filter. I laugh my ass off.

In another of the stories, Condorito shipwrecks on a remote island, finds a native with a parrot on his shoulder, thinks "A native! Surely these savages don't even know how to speak. Let's see," and then actually talks to the native and asks him the name of the parrot, only for the native to answer "Marilyn Monroe," making Condorito fall on his back, feet extended, like dropping dead with a dramatic *Plop!* Today, it seems racist, but back then, in that horrible line, with so many nervous and angry people, I laugh hard. Mother comes over, rips the magazine away from my hands, and puts it back.

"No more of this filth! Never again, you hear me?"

"Yes, Ma'am," but in my head I scream "Die, you fuckin' whore."

We finally get to the cashier and Mom places everything on the conveyor belt, except the Payco vanilla ice cream bucket that I had put on the cart.

"Why?"

"You need to learn. No more mundane stuff for you, and I mean it."

"Woman, *I demand an explanation!*" I joke with the most famous line of the comic strip, but she doesn't get it, and instead, I get a public slap for sassing her.

On Saturdays, Mother wakes me up early to get ready to preach from house to house with the rest of the brothers and sisters from the congregation. I hate it. I hate Mother for forcing me to do this. I hate going from house-to-house preaching stuff I don't care about to people who simply want to sleep in. I hate the heat. I hate the elder pushing me to distribute the

Watchtower and *Awake!* magazines and then have the gall to ask for donations. It's a sale game, but we are forbidden to call it that. I hate the whole lot of them, and it shows.

"Change your face, Pepe, or else," she would often say.

But I wouldn't change my face of disgust, of being utterly and absolutely lost, of not knowing why the hell was I sent to this world to such a disappointing family. And that face tends to propagate like an aerobic virus. A pandemic among the Jehovah's Witness youths. A California fire that cannot be quelled.

Just then, a Payco ice cream bus passes by. There is something wrong with the logo. The kid that appears in it is supposed to have a red cap, not a blue one. With its obnoxious slogan *Si no tiene la carita, no es Payco de verdad* ("If it doesn't have the little face is not really Payco") repeated ad nauseam, I am zombified and start asking Mother over and over for an orange cream ice pop.

"It's so hot, why do you punish me this way?" I scream when she refuses, at the top of my lungs, so that all the residents can hear me and see what this bitch is doing to me. "*I demand an explanation!*"

"Take him home, sister," the elder tells Mother. "And discipline him for his own sake."

That usually means that I'll spend the rest of my weekend confined to the walls of my room. Since this happens every Saturday from my tender age of 4 until I hit 14, I spend an entire decade grounded. I miss ten years of annual celebrations: Three Kings' Day, Easter, St. Valentine's, St. Patrick's, Halloween, Thanksgiving, and Christmas, ten years of birthdays, and I also miss all the normal milestones: first kiss, first girlfriend, first movie at a theater, first driving lessons, first everything. This is how normal growth is taken from me. This is how I am set out to be an outcast. Mother takes it all away from me. There's only the few *Condoritos* I borrow from my classmates and the tree house.

When Dad was alive, he was way more chill than Mother. And she was too. He made her laugh, tickling her every time he passed her by, throwing a kiss her way every few hours, getting worried sick whenever she took time getting back home from the market... He passes away on my tenth birthday. An undetected cancer goes rampant all over his body. If Mother never wanted me to celebrate my birthday, now

I'll never do. Before he dies, however, he builds me the tree house, and a hidden compartment to hide whatever I wanted from Mother's insidious eyes. That's where I put the *Condoritos* I borrow from my classmates, along with the porn playing cards, the dick-shaped candy, and the erotica novels that I stole from the municipal library.

The first time I jack off, it's to Yayita, Condorito's voluptuous human girlfriend. The first time I read the comic, I find the transspecies stuff a bit weird, but then, I am like "well, if it's such a popular comic strip, it must be normal." Yayita's huge tits, slim waist, and huge *culo* sends my sleeping hormones into a rage. I start touching myself over my jeans. This is pure instinct, because I don't know what the hell I'm doing, I just know it feels nice to rub my penis over my clothes, and it feels right. Pretty soon, I am humping the tree house floor, and it feels so right that I think something is going to happen down there, and just as whatever is about to happen happens, Mother's shrill-like voice echoes in the garden.

"Pepe, time for lunch! Get down here."

Helicopter cunt.

At age eleven, Dad gone and all, I start a new school.

"Hold on. I'm going with you."
"What?" I ask. "Why?"
"Be quiet and do as I say. Now come along."

I follow awkwardly as my mother moves her huge ass from side to side like a wrecking ball. I don't want anyone to identify me as her son.

"In here, now. Move along," she orders, while some 8th graders laugh and giggle at me.

Don't go red, don't go red, don't go red, I say to myself.

Inside await the Principal, the Social Worker, and the School Counselor.

"So, as I was saying, we are Jehovah's Witnesses."

Several eyebrows are raised high.

"As such, my son cannot participate in mundane activities and observance of holidays, like [...insert the long list here...] and, in case of medical emergency, he cannot receive blood transfusions."

"I'm sorry, what?" asks the Social Worker, shifting in her seat.

"I think Mrs. Gómez's concern here," the principal interjects, "is the spiritual wellbeing of her son, as well as the physical one. We understand," he sentences with a smile that appeases the other two. "Let's hope we don't ever have a situation that comes to that."

The principal takes Mother and I to my home classroom, to talk to the guy who will be my main teacher, Mr. Rivera, math and science teacher with a strong and deep connection to the outdoors and also head of the Boy Scouts' local chapter. Mother repeats to him the same litany she had ejaculated before at the principal's office. My will-be classmates hear everything. More raised brows. I'm starting to hate raised eyebrows.

"Ok, my job here is done. Now, be good," she tells me, but I don't even acknowledge her presence.

"Pepe, I'm talking to you."

But I don't answer. She doesn't exist to me, even if she feeds me. I don't feel anything towards this woman, except disappointment. Why did *she* have to be the one to bring me to this world?

She keeps talking to me, trying to make me react. Only when she leaves in frustration do I exhale.

"Pay no mind to that psycho," I tell everyone in class. "She's my kidnapper." *Plop!* Everyone laughs, including Mr. Rivera.

I try to make friends, but the culture doesn't help. It is customary, for instance, to invite your friends over for homework, play dates, videogame dates, sleepovers, and parties, but when you are a kid in a cult —or a cult kid, like some call me, though not to my face—, you are separated from the rest of the world, sometimes forcibly, sometimes through the us-vs-them language, like the way JWs call everyone else heathens or mundanes. *Mundies* for short, and in a very derogatory way. I cannot invite anyone home because I am grounded for a decade.

One day, the Payco ice cream bus with the wrong logo passes by my school. Several kids buy ice creams and come back inside. Some parents buy ice creams for their kids. And amidst the ruckus, no one notices when little Carlitos Walters Miranda has gone missing, his blue Spongebob Squarepants ironic and self-referential backpack lying on the floor.

"You are so not going outside ever again in your life," Mother says after the news of the kidnapping appear on TV.

"You never let me out anyway. When I die, they won't even find me. You'll have erased me."

She mutters some "rotten brat" nonsense and I go to my room to spend the hours looking at the walls and the ceiling. On her way to the bathroom, she stops by.

"You're bored because you want to," she spits at me just because she has the power

75

to do so. "You can spend the hours reading the Bible. Maybe you'll learn something."

Cultist cunt.

I escape my room through the window, climb a tree branch, and step into the tree house. If I leave right now, this is what I'll miss most. This place here. This is my real house. The one Dad made for me.

That year, seventeen boys disappear. They are all my age. Some are Latinos, like me. Some are black, very few are white. Panic ensues all over the city and the Island. Both the Mayor and the Governor are all over the press, assuring the good people of Puerto Rico that everything is ok, that everything will be fine, that the kidnapper will be caught, that they are doing everything in their power to get to him, and that the authorities are even considering bringing the FBI in on the manhunt.

I really don't give a fuck. I just want to leave this horrible woman.

One day, the 18th kid disappears, and he is in home classroom with me. His name is Alex Martínez. Mr. Rivera is destroyed. He can barely hold his speech together, and some of the girls are crying.

Someone hands me a paper note.

"We have been watching you. You look like a tough mutherfucker. We need you."

I turn to look, and two girls and a boy are looking straight at me with a face that reads like *We need to talk*.

At lunch break, they approach me.

"Pepe Gómez," says the boy. His name is Mark González.

"S'up?" I reply.

"Yeah, fuck this bullshit," says Delaine, the blonde of the girls. "Alex is our friend, and we want him back."

"What's your plan?" I ask.

"Sofía here," Mark says, pointing at the other girl, the silent one in the yellow hoodie over her plaid uniform skirt, "has an interesting theory. She believes the Payco ice cream bus is connected."

She explains her theory several times because she speaks in a very low voice, and it's difficult to hear her. But when she finally does, it all fits together. She says she has seen the Payco ice cream bus every single time there has been a disappearance. She also says there is a rhythm to its routes.

"So, we wait for him and follow in our bikes," she whispers. "If the Payco man is innocent, we just leave and that's that."

"I'm in," I say without further ado.

According to Sofía, the Payco bus was supposed to pass right in front of my house at 12:30 noon. And it does, like clockwork. My friends and I wait hidden behind some wild bougainvillea bushes in full multicolor bloom. The baskets on our bikes are loaded with plastic bags.

"Wait until he's at the corner," Delaine commands. "Now!"

We start pedaling because the neighborhood ends there, at the corner, and that's when he'll accelerate and, if we're not quick enough, we'll lose him. And true enough, we almost lose him at the intersection between the new road and the old one. He turns right and we're careful enough to stay in his blindside, until he reaches an unmarked point on the road and makes a turn into the unpaved bush. At some point, we jump into a trench for cover, because there's a barn, smack in the middle of nowhere, and the Payco bus driver is slowing down. We hide well under the tall dry grasses.

From my vantage point, I spy as the driver gets off the bus, walks towards the entrance of the barn, which is painted in a kind of golden beige, I guess in order to camouflage it. In he goes and locks after.

"Let's move," Delaine says, but Sofía is already crouching and lurking at the window of the barn. We pass by the ice cream bus on our way there. We were right. The brand is all wrong. The boy in the logo is not freckled like the Payco boy is supposed to be. And his baseball cap is blue, not red like normally. It looks slightly bootlegged.

We reach Sofía and listen in silence. Soon, we detect muffled screams, long shrilling screams gagged by some clothe. I brave a glimpse. There's Alex, naked, his legs up and tied to the ceiling, his arms tied behind his back, silenced by a black t-shirt around his mouth, the driver impaling him with something. A finger? A fist?

The kid screams one final time and goes silent. From where I am, I see he just faints. And I spot a bloodied knife exiting him. And gashes. So many gashes all over his body, like deep trenches in a forgotten war. I nearly throw up.

"Alex... is in pretty bad shape," I am able to say.

"Here," Sofía handles Mark a shank made by constantly and furiously rubbing a silver spoon against cement to form a makeshift dagger. "Go punch holes in his tires."

"What are you gonna do?" I ask.

"Delaine and I will make a diversion. You set Alex free."

They grab glass bottles with a yellowish liquid from the plastic bags. And a lighter. They torch them and throw them at one of the back windows. They ignite immediately. The man runs out of the door, where Mark intercepts him with a crowbar. He falls down immediately with a sound *Plop!*

"Tie him up," I say before I sprint inside to save Alex. I run, cut out his ropes with the bloodied knife that the driver left on the table, grab him, and walk him out, naked and bloodied as he is.

Sofía and Delaine are waiting outside with a blanket, with which they cover Alex's modesty. Meanwhile, a quiet but huge ball of fire engulfs the barn, sending a huge smoke signal to the authorities.

When the cops arrive, we tell them everything. They authorities inspect the entire area, but they find nothing until Alex comes out of his shell at the last minute and speaks.

"Look under the barn," he says before fainting.

Under a floor latch, now noticeable due to its current state of charring, they find the stuff of nightmares.

"You are gonna want to see this," one police officer tells another.

"What is it?" I ask.

"Shh, come on, kid," he says, meaning *haven't you seen and done enough?* But I have to know. I have to see. I must see.

"*I demand an explanation*," is all I say, and the police officer rolls his eyes and lets me pass.

What I see will be with me forever: a common grave with more than fifty dead boys.

Sofía starts crying. Delaine consoles her. Mark is livid. And so am I. The driver wakes up. He's cuffed but I don't care. I pick up the first stone I find.

"Hey, kid. What the hell do you think you're doing?!" cries one cop, but the other stops him with a hand and a shake of his head from side to side.

Mark, Delaine, and Sofía pick up stones in both hands. Big ass stones. This is for innocence. This is for children. This is for us. The stones hit him all in the head at the same time. He falls on his back, feet up. His final *Plop!*

A Month with James Franco

Beck Gilfoyle looks up from his tawny wood desk at the place he has rented for his startup and catches a glimpse of the ad on the TV. It features a bare-chested James Franco, smiling high as nuts at the camera, announcing a workshop slash retreat slash getaway (his words). For prices and payment plans, call 1-888-IAM-HIGH.

"Oh, God. Is he still even alive?" comments Margaret, the secretary.

"Apparently so," Beck answers, feigning disinterest.

But a month with James Franco sounds like the kind of gig he needs to rekindle his acting career. He waits for Margaret to join the others at the conference room. The meeting to decide the fate of Ringai, his app, is about to start. He looks at the ceiling. Industrial, with the plumbing hanging exposed, like the building's bare balls. Like *Le Centre Pompidou*. High ceilings to breathe easily. Walls and ceiling white. Everything white in and out. Cheapest color to paint a building. Hides imperfections well. Allows for the illusion of big space. What will I say to the investors? Beck wonders. And then, he gets up and faces destiny.

"Good morning," he greets those at the meeting.

Margaret winks at him and mimics clapping silently with her hands, meaning that his black suit fits like a dream, his hair is sleek and impeccable, his tie in Eldredge knot is on point, and his shoes shine just like his youthful hopes. He looks like a million dollars. Margaret keeps him in check. She's the only one who knows how to short-circuit his neurodivergence. She understands him. She's like his own personal safe space.

"So, during our first week, Ringai saw sales in the billions. As predicted," he says, making sure to stress "predicted" just the right tad, "sales really skyrocketed in the fourth weeks, which is amazing, and also as predicted, they plummeted after the first month."

"Well, the app is ridiculous," Phillip interjects. He's one of the shareholders, the white one with the hipster beard.

"Phillip, healthy interactions only, please," Margaret interrupts.

"I don't mean it in a bad way. I mean, using AI to analyze people's voice recordings and messages to make melodies and remixes out of it? It's ridiculous. What did y'all expect?"

"Well, as I said before," Beck states curtly, trying not to show his roll of eyes, "this was predicted. We planned for this. Second month sees the release of the first paid extension of the app. We foresee going back to the billions in the first week."

"And our dividends for the first month?" asks a platinum blonde with reddish night makeup in the full of day.

"Margaret?"

His secretary, an Asian woman clad in a poignant and edgy white leather blazer, and a rose tube skirt, stands up and distributes sealed envelopes with checks in them.

"Perfect. See you next month," she says, and with her, several other investors stand up and leave.

"Great," Beck sighs, while Margaret pats him on his back.

"God knows you try," she says, and he smiles.

"God knows I try. Hey, Phillip," he interrupts, calling after the white bearded hipster. "How'd you like to buy me out?"

When you thought you were alone in the world, along came 3 friends from your own same flock, and together, nerds united, you shall conquer the world!

The intro song is idiotic, but effective and way catchier than it looks on paper. The sitcom is called *UnSTEM!* and is about four friends who are Humanities nerds:

Daniela (Dani) Reyes, a Latina who graduated from Art History and works in a museum; Janice Ian, a Lebanese American who graduated from Art and is always at odds with Dani, she works as a brand consultant; Cooper Brooks, a philosophy grad and the grumpy one, who works for a German car company as the HR boss; and Feiyu Liu, a Chinese expert in Ayn Rand who waits tables at Zuko's.

The scene opens with Janice talking on the phone. The audience claps and whistles like the actress is Courtney Cox or Jennifer Aniston, except she's not and you can tell that the fluffers are working that audience hard.

"Yes, hon, see, this is the thing... yup... right? Sure thing, you'll have it by Monday first light. Bye bye."

"Who was that?" asks Dani, who enters through the blue and bright yellow kitchen, which is to the right of the living room, where most of the Pilot takes place. The audience claps harder, like the actress is Jennifer Lopez and not some Juanita Pérez from the literal *culo* of the world.

"No idea," Janice answers. The audience laughs. "Hey, what are we eating tonight?"

"Right, tonight is my turn to choose."

"Please not Spicy Jenny again!" Janice exclaims.

"Please not Spicy Jenny again!" Cooper exclaims, making his first entrance on the show. The audience goes wild for the white straight guy, played by Beck. They laugh and clap like seals at an aquarium. "Last week you gave me a 'rhoids the size of JLo's ass." The audience laughs but oohs too. "I was able to sit again today. Don't take that away from me." The public goes wild.

"Oh, you, poor white guy," answers Feiyu, making his entrance and completing the foursome. The audience fangirls and claps hard because the actor is Ken Jeong, the Chinese guy from *The Hangover*. "Oh, I can't," he says, literally tearing his uniform apart, dropping his pants, and collapsing on the couch in his boxers. He looks like he worked so much that he overheated. The audience laughs as if being tickled on their kinky parts. No one will know just how much this scene takes of them, especially the toll that acting takes on Beck.

The appointed date comes, and the taxi stops in front of a white, two-story 1920 Spanish villa, right across the street from the super famous Chateau Marmont in West Hollywood. A young, shaggy white dude with sparse chin hair and mustache greets Beck in a white bathrobe and pajamas, his Sad Sam eyes locked in an impish, half-baked smile.

Yup, you're definitely here to make friends and contacts, Beck thinks. *What can this boy actually teach me?*

"Hey, man. Welcome to my humble abode," he says, greeting me with a hug as warm as $3,000,000, which is what the retreat costs per head.

"Thank you," Beck says just as warmly.

"You're Beck Gilfoyle, right? Aren't you the Ringai guy?"

Better to be recognized for Ringai than for UnSTEM! Beck thinks.

"Urgh, yup."

"Oh, we so have to talk, man. But listen, I want you to feel free, to disconnect this month, we have a pool, a garden to hang out, all the weed you can imagine... Want a puff?" he asks, offering Beck a go at his Northern Lights Indica joint.

"Indica makes me sick. I'm a Sativa guy," Beck replies.

"Well, then, try this *other* one," James Franco says, producing another joint from his pocket as if by magic. "One rule, though. No cellphones this month," he says, while we approach his butler, a tall, burly black man with a face that screams no patience for bullshit.

The Pilot is a huge success, so the network orders an entire 32-episode first season. The situations include all sorts of different scenarios: Halloween with Dani as Frida Kahlo with a huge chola unibrow, Janice and Dani berating people obsessed with sports at the museum's employee appreciation field day. Cooper trying to play the fiddle in Christmas while Feiyu puts a fiddle playback record, making him believe that he actually has some talent, and this leading to a disastrous *America's Got Talent* presentation... Situation after funny situation, inspired, of course, by *The Big Bang Theory*, but in a Humanities setting. Memes flourish among the Internet society, particularly with Cooper, the autistic character reminiscent of Sheldon; the actors appear on several interviews and talk shows promoting *UnSTEM!*, and the show solidifies its identity in popular culture. When talks about renewing for a second season start, however, only silence fills the void. The network calls the actors, directors, and producers to a big meeting, and makes them fill out non-disclosure agreements.

Beck meets the others: Matsuri, a girl whose parents survived jap internment camps in the West Coast during WWII and who starred in a Pilot playing a robotic nanny girl; Kellx, a nonbinary gothic lolito from Berlin, who starred in a historic spy-vs-spy dramedy set during the Cold War, and Jacob, a white dude who started doing voice acting thinking he could pull a Mae Whitman and do the crossover to life action acting. All losers like him, who got booted by Hollywood because their shows were not oomph enough. They hang out together for like a few minutes until the pills, the weed, and the Robitussin kick in. James Franco does some ice-breaking dynamics with the foursome, and then puts his speedo on and dives in his pool.

"Come on, guys!"

His butler comes around with a machine vaporizer that looks like one of those T-shirt bazookas at rock concerts. He puts in a suspicious mix of weed and dried magic shrooms and spits out wild white curls of gossamer smoke that transform the house into a breathing entity that vibrates with each of their synched respiration patterns. They all join hands in a circle at some point and sing *Love casinos, Indian reservations, but, baby, if you love me, take me to the gas station*, and pass out running like Naruto ninjas, and laughing at stupid shapes in the clouds that look like Ted Cruz, the most punchable face in America.

That month, so much shit happens. They smoke a lot of different strains of weed. They each get eight 6-packs of Gatorade in their rooms, lots of water bottles, candies, and assorted nuts. A bunch of topless girls come visit Franco one afternoon, play in the pool with the guys from the retreat, and then have sex with Franco, Seth Rogen, and Judd Apatow, who are also invitees. And his butler, of course.

They do so many acting exercises that they lose the count, like screaming at each other while playing water polo, Matsuri and Kellx piggybacking on Beck and Jacob's shoulders, or like making ceramics with a clay turner while imagining being the seducer in a love triangle gone wrong suspense flick, or like playing hide and seek while imagining that they are in an alien abduction scene. Or weird and really childish stuff like playing Real World (forcing confrontations for confrontation's sake) or passing around a secret by whispering it in each other's ears, several times in a cycle, until absolutely nothing remains of the original message (which was "Jared Leto is a turd," and somehow ended up being "Gwyneth Paltrow was unfaithful"). There's also a Thursday afternoon session called "Healthy Sauna Interactions in a Yurt." And they top off every day of activities with ridiculous frappés of just two blueberries, two raspberries, two strawberries, water, and ice, the recipe for which James Franco got from Kate Hudson.

But the most important part, at least for Beck, is the parties, which don't always end up in orgies, but most do. The first one happens on the 4th day. He invites the usual two: Rogen and Apatow, but there's also Jared Leto, Jay Baruchel, Danny McBride, Emma Watson, Emma Stone, Jonah Hill, Marilyn Manson, Chris Pratt, Josh Duhamel, and so many limelight and backstage stars that the force of gravity weighs heavy on him. He has never done good at parties. Too many stimuli. So, instead, he decides to watch and make mental notes as to who fucks who. To his surprise, several casual homosexual encounters do take place while everyone is half baked. *This information may come in handy*, he surprises himself thinking. Beck *Gilfoyle, how dare you! You're not like that!* he chastises himself and tries to flow. The next morning, a very erect, drunk, and high James Franco makes a pass at Matsuri and Emma Stone, both of whom laugh it off, as they are still drunk and high as fuck as well. The girls end up pushing him into the pool, where he pisses himself, leaving a very deep blue stain in the water around him.

"Gross," Emma Stone says and dives into it.

"Ew indeed," sentences Matsuri as she follows suit.

After the NDA, things only get worse for Beck. With no show, there is no more Ig Lives, no more invitations to Comic Cons or interviews in late-night shows like Conan O'Brien. After all, a cancelled show is a lost show, a foul. A *box-office bomb*, that's the term. And everybody knows that a box-office bomb cast is a cursed cast.

He loses touch with his fellow cast members, even with Kim Jeong, who no longer remembers him. The actresses who played Janice and Dani go back to waiting tables at some obscure diner franchise in Emeryville and Modesto, their respective towns. Even the director goes into hiding. The producers had told him off before the start of the first and only season, one of those "you fail me, and you'll never work in this town again."

That happens almost in the first days of summer 2010. And if shitty stuff like this happens at the beginning of the most free and magical season, then that year, summer will be a bummer. That's when he meets Margaret at a Sillicon Valley thinktank. They quickly come up with the idea of an app that uses AI to purchase en masse audio data from people's mobiles and create ringtones, like Gavin Newsom rapping Eminem's "Love the Way You Lie," or Donald Trump backdropping his "You're fired" to Katy Perry's "Teenage Dream." And as expected, the stupid app sells like hot cakes.

There comes the Poker night.
"Alright guys, you know the drill," James Franco says. "This exercise is to eliminate tells and improve your poker face. I'll be your dealer tonight. And always…" he says and giggles like a dumb, horny, and stoned teenager. Everyone sits down and gets ready, and James deals the first hand. As it progresses, the butler attempts to drive the conversation, guided meditation style, with background harp tunes.

Beck focuses solely on his cards and on studying everyone else. His only chance is to make it obvious that everyone else is his guinea pig and that he's the scientist. His usual tactics at public settings and gatherings. His shield. Matsuri's tells are obvious. Whenever she has shitty cards or a losing hand, she carelessly brushes a strand of hair off her face back behind her ear. When she's packing, she rubs her right eye. Jacob's tells are more difficult to detect. He has been playing since kindergarten. But he has a rhythm. He cycles and recycles his tells. And once Beck discovers those five recycled tells, Jacob is toast. Then, there is Kellx, the nonbinary amoeba, as Beck calls him inside his mind. Kellx has the most difficult tells, because he dresses as a woman and uses woman tells that throw him off. He doesn't like trans people or nonbinaries. Their very existence drowns him in cognitive dissonance. The presence of just one of the Pronoun People, as Margaret calls them, sends wave after wave of OCD questions, like, *how can one be nonbinary when no one can escape the binary, let alone any binary at all? What is gender identity and why doesn't he have one? Why does transfeminist discourse feels like playing along or pretending? In what universe is a trans woman the same as a woman? In what universe is it ok for trans kids to even exist, and why are they allowed to transition when they have not finished forming as what they were born as? In what universe do trans rights not erase women's rights? How is being a trans woman not woman face? In what universe is a lesbian a transphobe for refusing to suck a trans woman's dick? Am I a transphobe for thinking like this?* It would always be like this, a pure assault of questions that could never be answered for fear of retribution, cancelling, and so much more bullshit. But Beck has been experiencing this Niagara of questions ever since he met Kellx. So far, he had avoided the dude with one black and one blond eyebrow, dressed in oversized sheer skirts and shirts that barely covers an ass clad in white laced lingerie while sporting the most stupid Polish mustache. He hates Kellx, definitely. Not because Kellx is nonbinary. But because of the cognitive dissonance. Kellx is his reminder that cultish people are taking over.

"Are you ok, hun?" Kellx asks.

"Shut up and play," is Beck's only response, all the while thinking that there really must be a way to defeat this asshole. And then, he spots it. The one tell that is above all tells: his arched eyebrow when he's packing. Beck pounces and wins the game.

"Now, look at you! Underdog!" exclaims James Franco, hugging and showering Beck in cheap glitter. And it's actually then when time slows down, while the glitter is falling on him, while James's mouth is open in a gesture induced by chemical euphoria, Beck finally understands that this has been a huge waste of time, an overload of stimuli for someone like him, an almost month of bullshit that will get him nowhere. Yeah, it's all in the cheap ass glitter.

Beck stands up curtly. James Franco and all those present are shaken into silence.

"Sass up," is the only thing to exit Franco's lips.

"What the fuck have I been thinking?" is Beck's sole response.

He doesn't say shit after that. He just walks to the room he had been staying in, packs all his stuff back into his suitcase, gets out of James Franco's certified nuthouse, and drives away from Sunset Boulevard, away from Palo Alto, the hell away from Los Angeles and Silicon Valley. And California. "Fuck California," he says, as he drives north. Oregon, maybe? Who cares. California is simply a lost cause.

Antiaris toxicaria var. ultimata

The Court is silent. The man in the white rolled boucle wig sits on the bench, his black toga caressing his legs, his look stern, like a caring father trying to refrain from applying strict discipline to his only child. The people are equally clad in black, as the occasion demands. Only Tike is dressed in white.

"Mister Foreman, how does the Jury find the defendant?" the Judge asks.

"Your Honor, we find the defendant guilty on the counts of lying with other men."

"Thank you, Mister Foreman. The accused, having been found guilty, is hereby sentenced to work the Upas field for five months or until he expires."

"No! Not the Upas field!" cries a woman, presumably the young man's mother.

"Your Honor, please. We ask for leniency," supplicates the father on bended knees.

"Silence!" the judge shouts.

A man rises from his seat with elegance and grace. He is the best dressed person in the whole courtroom, his waistcoat and trousers spotless and immaculately charcoal, his ascot olive green, shining gold spectacles, blue eyes, and handsome ginger moustache in Russian loops. He stands regally, black, silver, and cobalt cane in his right hand.

"Your Honor. The Upas field is a death sentence. I believe this young man could better suit the society he failed by serving hard labor in my mansion. He would work hard and get an education that would deter his behavior."

"I thank you, Lord Manning, but my sentence is final and unappealable. However, I shall amend it to two weeks, following recovery, education, and hard labor at your residence, should he survive."

"Thank you, Peace Justice Brannagh."

The young man, whose hair and clothes are shabby and dirty, looks at Lord Manning with a twisted and confused look of gratitude. Lord Manning does not look back.

The boy is taken by the guards to the chariot that will lead him to the field, a ten square acre land plot full of Upas trees and a rundown hut to sleep in. Lord Manning arrives on his own horse.

"Nate, listen to me. They want you to harvest the latex of the Upas trees. You'll find the tools needed inside the hut. Whatever you do, take heed of two things: the latex of the trees is extremely poisonous. Do not let it touch you. Also, do not let it touch the earth. I will send food and drink for you twice a day. Now, be a good boy and try to survive. We will talk as soon as you get out of here."

"Lord Manning?"

"Yes, my dear boy?"

"Thank you, sir."

The look in Lord Manning's visage is as stern as the judge's yet seasoned with true concern.

"Loving another person constitutes neither sin nor crime. Unfortunately, we don't live alone. Society around us has arbitrarily decided that this kind of love is punishable by death. The worst and painfulmost death. You must endure, so you get to love again."

After a pause, he says: "Here. This will help pass the days."

With that, the lord gives Nathan a notebook clad in the most velvety red leather, several featherpens, and three bottles of ink. He grabs the young man's face with his left hand, and as they close their eyes, their foreheads meet in silence. Then, the soldiers close the barbed fence.

Day 1:

Lord Manning leaves in deep concern. I am ashamed. It's a good thing there are no mirrors here, as I cannot stand to look at my reflection.

I have wandered around the field. There is a lake close by. The water seems harmless, so I take off my clothes and bathe in it. I also take several sips and enjoy myself as best as I can. The solitude, though, is killing me. It's a silent assassin that could very well become a mute friend.

After I dry off in the breeze and the sun, I go inside the hut. The tools are there, so I start to work. A stick, a mallet, a wooden fan-shaped paddle, and several buckets to fill and deliver to the soldiers at the end of each day.

I climb the small hill and get to the first Upas tree. Its leaves are a dark green that could easily be confused with black. I caress the bark, taking care not to scratch it unwittingly, and looking for possible openings where the tree would let go of its sap. Latex is not sap. The extraction technique is different, as sap is located somewhere else in the tree. Lord Manning tells me that before he leaves. Before we touch foreheads. I cry a bit. I don't understand any of this.

No one gives me clear instructions as to how to do this without dying. Perhaps they want me to fail and die. Lord Manning gives me clues, though. Use the mallet to hammer the wooden stick deep into the bark. Place the paddle and gently lift it sixty degrees up and put the bucket underneath to receive the latex. It comes down gently, and I thought, what a shame that such a white, gummy, and elastic substance can kill with a mere touch. The bucket fills gently. I watch from afar, sitting on a grass bed that is still green. Curious thing about the Upas Trees: nothing really grows around them. On the other hand, what little grows turns black and dies, but remains, a corpse or a ghost of what could have been. The bucket takes the entire afternoon to fill, and it is nearly ready by the time the soldiers arrive.

"Oi, are you done with that shite?"

"Here you go, sir."

"Don't sir me, you faggot. Now off with you. Here. This be your payment, from Lord Manning."

They give me a 4-tier Indian tiffin box, a letter, and a bottle of wine. I open the letter and read.

My beautiful boy:

My heart lies broken, shattered, asunder, as if lighting itself had befallen me, like a curse. Losing you, even two weeks, is too much. Take heed of Lord Manning's advice. Follow all his instructions and you'll be fine. Trust that your father and I love you very much, even if the whole world claims for your blood.

Loving you dearly,

Mom
I can't help it. I cry myself to sleep.

Day 4:

It's easy to cry these days. The loneliness is killing me. I've tried to escape the field but its barbed all around, even the limits of the lake. It feels empty. I feel empty. Birds won't land here. Not even ants make their building in this earth. And the soldiers have been demanding four buckets daily.

Last night I received a letter from Lord Manning. He gives me tricks and exercises to keep myself sane during this ordeal. Jumping jacks, lunges, squats, and other calisthenics I do because he asks. But mostly, he begs me to exercise my imagination. "Populate the field with your mind." And as such, I touch myself today, for the first time since I came here. I walk all the way to the riverbed, take my clothes off, gently hump the soil, and finger my behind. I think of you, my Lord. Only you can save me.

Day 9:

The task has grown easy on me. Or perhaps I rise to it. I can fill buckets quicker and I've already developed a delivery system with a small bamboo pole and two buckets at each side. I haven't spilled Upas latex on the land. And I haven't gotten it into my clothes or on my skin.

Father sends me a letter advising against opening my skin. Beware of insect bites, he says. Beware of stings, cuts, bruises. Don't eat wild berries. Beware of this, don't do that... His way of loving is so dry, yet so abundant, at times, his words feel like waves of dunes, or tornados of sand that somehow manage to get into my throat, leaving it dry and without access to speech.

Nevertheless, I silently obey. Silence, that's in surplus here, a deafening continuous wave of nothing. I confess I only remember language when I sit here to write. Outside this hut, I'm a savage, a hill-dweller, a condemned man who lies with other men. In the silence, only your voice, Lord Manning. Your voice as light, sir, a firefly in shadowland. Come for me, sir. Please, rescue me.

Day 10:

I stay in the shadows most of the day. The sky is clear for the first time this year. I have never seen such blue in the heavens above. I think I could fly away, like one of those ravens that visit dangerous omens upon us mortals. Fly to Valhalla, the Elysian Fields, Eden... The dark green can get to you, but the blue, the blue is welcoming until the sun irradiates its unbearable heat like a kiss of doom. I'm tired today, more than usual. Lord Manning sends me bread, cheese, and fruit juice for breakfast. Face down on the ground, I can almost fit my entire hand inside thinking of him. In my imagination, the one he implores me to use in order to inhabit this never-ending field, he penetrates me. He takes me from behind, pushes me against the ground until he crushes me with his immense weight. He takes his time inside. Hours go by, and while he squashes me with his incredible frame, I endure, because he says he loves me, and all I need are those three words to feel I'm part of some forgotten benign force in this universe that I fail to understand, no matter how much I try.

I prepare. I am ready. He will take me; he will own me. He won't have to brand me. I will willingly brand myself his slave.

Day 12:

Today it finally happens. I bleed the final tree and a drop of latex falls on my cheek. It starts burning immediately. I take off all my clothes and run towards the lake. I clean most of it, but a nasty black stain appears on my face. I can see it on the water's reflection.

That night, when the soldiers come, they're pissed. I only have one bucket, out of the four they demanded.

"What the hell happened to you, bastard?" one of them asks.

"It looks like he finally got some on his face. Funny, you look."

"You know what would cure it? A bit of my spunk," he says while he grabs his crotch and roars with laughter.

I withdraw while giving them the two fingers, but they follow, ambush me, hold me down, and have their way with me.

"Be quiet, you little shite, or I'll plunge your head into the bucket. Would you like that?"

No, I wouldn't, and though it hurts, I let them penetrate and fist me. And soon, they are done all over my face. It feels warm and sticky, and I leave it there. The lake water is too cold a bath and if the poison doesn't melt half my face, the cold water will finish me off during the night. Once again, I cry myself to sleep.

Final day:

Today is the last day of my punishment. Lord Manning himself appears at the gates of the Upas field. I am so happy that my erection shows underneath my ravaged clothes. He only smiles, then embraces me. He places a soft finger on the damage the latex had done to my cheek.

"Nothing that can't be remedied with rose and lavender ointment."

He kisses my forehead, and dresses me in clothes as fine as his. There is silver thread in black trousers and waistcoat, a silver chain watch, and chrysanthemum perfume.

"Lovely," he says and bids me to climb on his horse. He takes a slow pace but holds me close all the same. I am beside myself, all the trip imagining him inside. My erection hurts, but it's okay. I am saved.

That night, Lord Manning leaves town on a caravan of horses and chariots. He moves his property to Sallery, a hamlet hidden between a waterfall and a forest. There are only two roads in and out of Sallery, and Nathan knows them well. He also knows he won't need them, as there's no branding awaiting him, just strict education, tough daylight love, and a warm bed with two pillows.

Freaky Bloody Katana

> *"did you honestly think it would be that easy?"*
> *"you know what? For a moment there? Yeah, I kinda did."*
> *"silly rabbit..."*
> *"trix are for kids..."*
> **Kill Bill**

> *Bugger this. I want a better world.*
> **Epitaph on Jenny Sparks' grave, from the comic series**
> ***The Authority***

I. Showdown at the Dorms

There. I knew it would come to this someday. Some years have passed since I purchased this *katana* at the black market on Malén St. Right now, it may be the first time it tastes blood. It may. I'm standing right in front of an amused terrorist, obviously well trained in martial arts. I'm standing posed in the *gatoutsu* way: right leg behind, right knee bent 55° (that's the secret), left leg set at the front, also bent, but more slightly so the impulse of the right leg won't disturb it, on the contrary, so it will augment the force of the legwork; my right hand, the one holding the *katana* is also bent, pointing the sword to the front, arching it 35° towards my opponent, my left fingers stretched to the front, almost caressing the pointy-edged tip. I feel gorgeous and terrible (and a little guilty for feeling that way), as if just with my stance I had power over life and death, imbuing the whole scene with my will and my never-blinking eyes, the eyes of a warrior never leaving the opponent's. The silence is upon us like the veil that falls over a war field where two kings are to personally face each other under a stormy night. Even those wounded feel it, and I notice they're in awe, not that I really see them, rather captured their feelings with the corner of my eyes. It cannot be more perfect. I knew it would be like this.

"Finally. Someone with dignity enough to face me. Or a measure of dignity whatsoever..." the terrorist says. "Hey, hold on a minute... do we know each other?"

"Yeah, that we do, bitch." I spit. "Your goon robbed me at work, at the store, a few months ago, remember now? Bastard. Do you think you can talk about dignity? Do you see yourself in such high regard, Elvin? Fuck you! You've no right to talk about no fuckin' dignity! Assaulting those who got no money to eat. Killing and dismembering innocent men and women! Fuck your ideals! You're nothing! Your little bigot terror ends now!"

"My, my. Such high words coming from such a brat! Perhaps you should demonstrate some of what makes you so cocky."

"I will. I'll also make sure those hands never dismember anyone ever again."

I focus all my anger on those words, sending my warrior spirit towards him like waves of breeze that caress his hair and make him tremble for a fragment of seconds. I can smell fear in his eyes, even if his poker face is solid. There is silence still. I can feel the leaves falling down, as everything my eyes gazes upon turns to red, black, and white. Then, with the caw of a black bird my nerves tense my legs, and I spring, running towards him the samurai way: foot after foot in single line, no more space between them than an inch. When I reach his surprised face, I thrust my sword in a very beautiful movement that concludes the *gatoutsu*: it looks more like a fencing movement than a samurai sword technique, but then my right arm is at the back no more, but completely extended as I dash into him with the last impulse of my hip.

II. First finale

When the tip of my sword almost reaches the left side of his chest, I decide that I don't really want to kill him. He's unworthy. So, at the last fraction of second, I flip my body completely around him, and used my sword like a bat, delivering a two handed blow with the blunt back of my sword, to the back of his head, in the very point where it connects with the neck. Such is the force of my blow that, for a moment, I doubt I ever hit him. But when I hear the single only bone cracking sound, I know he's done with. He falls on both knees, eyes opened to its sockets, mouth ajar and gargling, but he can't speak. It is over before it even began.

III. What if...?

When the tip of my sword almost reaches the left side of his chest, I decide not to kill him but to show him what happens to unmerciful people who use innocents to achieve their goals. Instead of piercing his heart, I raised my sword, and off goes the armed hand, the right one. A geyser of blood gushes out of the clean wound. I am somewhat surprised at the way my sword goes through his flesh and bone, as if it was nothing more than mere butter or silk. I am high on that feeling, so I deliver suffering onto my opponent, slashing out his left eye, slitting his smile open to both his ears, taking a finger here, a toe there, a foot tendon, the whole left arm, and half a leg with its knee cap. It is over in less than five seconds. He lies there screaming so high that it's almost imperceptible to human ears, five or six fountains of blood sprouting from his body, as I stand before him, bathing in his blood, recovering my lost mercy and virtue, and looking down at the body of punishment, mutilated by the sword that defends the innocent, the sword of rightfulness.

IV. Same Ending

"Your punishment has been served, mister. Withdraw your troops and get the Hell out of here. If not, I will keep taking parts of your body, and I promise you this: you are going to miss them far more than the ones I already took."

Some of his men, those who are able to recover from the shock of watching their General on his knees, make to his aid, taking him in their arms the only way they can, almost without any care at all for the man they had followed all this long, their symbol taken down. I spit on the floor. This is the end of it. But I can't let them go without a final warning.

"General Plaud!"

They turn to me.

"Those were my friends whose lives you took back there! I won't ever forget that! You shouldn't either! So, run while you can."

V. Irreversible

I am shaking. I have never been in the middle of a terrorist attack before, and probably will never be. The student dorms are being attacked, floor by floor, by the extremist Belongers, a paramilitary group of clandestines who desperately want Puerto Rico to be part of the United States. I am terrified because I am not alone when the screams GRAND OLE COUNTRY OR DEATH! spreads out. Heather and Rosalina are with me. At first, we don't cry. I take my *katana*, the one I bought on Malén St., and take the girls with me to one of the restrooms on my floor, the one that is single. It's the perfect hideout, maybe because of the OUT OF SERVICE sign. There, in the darkness and the cold floor, we listen to the trained footsteps of what seem to be like ten or eleven of General Elvin Plaud's goons. I hear the screams of my neighbors, slain in cold with their girlfriends, a river of blood reaching the space between the restroom's door and the floor. By then, we are sobbing, but not too loud, until we more or less feel they are gone.

"Oh my God, Wyatt! There's... blood... they must be dead... all of them..."

"*Sshh*, Heather, easy," I try to console her but it's impossible, for I need the same calm I'm trying to give her and there's none to be found. The only calm available during tragedies like this is in the nerves of the slayers. "I'm gonna protect you guys, don't worry, I won't let anything happen to you," but even I can't believe those words. It's only when they go away that I risk the bathroom's light and see the actual river of red plasma, but also my *katana*, like really see it.

I've had it for four years already, and I've never taken a good look at it. All I really know about it is what the clerk lady tells. It was a Chirijiraden, which means it is supposed to cut like crazy, and some apocryphal Japanese legend says that Lord Chirijiraden made this sword at the close of one of the feudalist eras, and he imbued the blade with his spirit. *As long as you bathe in blood, your edge shall never dull nor be forgotten.* That same lady tells me that the Chirijiraden is a rare treasure from the Tokugawa era.

"See, the smith who made it made only one sword in his entire life. Only this one. He started at the tender age of 8, guided by his father. Every day of his life he worked on his blade a little bit. He finished it when he was 108. It took him a whole century to finish. And the result is this."

I think I take it for granted and never really give it a second thought. The handle alone is a thing of beauty, made of yellow-ochre-golden wood laced together with bright turquoise cords. It has a sapphire on the tip of the handle. The cords on the sheath are also turquoise and the wood is the same strange yellow color. As for the shield of the blade, it is round, with an odd sort of star. It is simply precious enough to be hope giving and inspiring.

"Rosalina, take the stairs with Heather to the 19th floor. Wait for me there."

"Please, promise me you'll be back."

"I'll try."

I open the door softly, trying not to reveal any creaking sound and lead the girls to the stairs. As I open the door, hopping over naked bodies that were not recognizable anymore, whether because of the piles of dismembered members or the bloody ocean all over the place, I reach the stairs' door and open it only to find more macabre stuff all over (oh, my god, is that Mara's head? Oh no, please no... it cannot be...). There are couples I knew and some that I did not, holding hands, some embracing (if they had members to do that); some of them holding their lover's head, or kissing without arms. It's horrible. Heather and Rosalina can't cry, we're simply too shocked. Our friends were just alive merely hours ago.

"Ok, go now!"

"Please, come back!"

"I will. I promise I will!"

I hear their footsteps as they clack against the concrete stairs, and the echo is amplified by the walls. As their sounds disappear, hopefully because they're already there, alive, I turn to the other direction. I begin the climb down and cannot help myself but gasp in awe and horror, as I see the girl from the second floor, the one in a wheelchair; she lies there naked, armless, at the edge of the stairs, crying but trying not to so loud as to not fall down (god, they left her alive, armless in a wheelchair...). I quickly go to her aid.

She was a beauty to behold. Mariana was her name, she had always been, a beauty on wheels, perfect in her own way. But now, her light brown, blow-dried-straight hair is curled red by the dye of her own blood. Both arms have been taken, but not clean. Some pieces of bone, skin and muscle still hang, as if they had been torn apart by a half-dull axe or a chainsaw. She turns to me as I drive her to safety. When I turn her around, I see an original trail of blood coming from her vagina. It has been cut open in the same manner. She keeps sobbing, but it's not fear. It's relief. I understand immediately and unsheathe my sword.

I leave Mariana and go down all the way to the lobby. I am careful enough not to make any sound. I need to know how much distance is left between me and the perpetrators. I hear footsteps, trained, rhythmic, in harmony. I dare open the door a little bit without risking it cringe. A voice rises over the rabble.

"Burn it to cinders! Let them burn!"

What a voice! I think. So commanding... it must be their general, sergeant, or leader. But it has the same certain cockiness that can freeze you down in your tracks, whether the owner has a weapon, or whether you have one, that voice is an instrument of real evil. I've read about it somewhere, natural born leaders have voices like that, it's called the warrior spirit, taking over the frequencies of your music box, doing the thinking for you, placing the statements in the right tone, with the right gestures and flexion, and with intention. His voice is like an orchestrated advertisement, full of subtleties and subliminal stuff. His voice says things in a very respectful manner, but what it really means can only be understood at a deeper level: *you better do as I say mutherfuckers or I'm gonna stick this gun up your fuckin' asses and shoot! Or even better, I'm going to TNT your asses and blow your brains out!* It's that kind of voice. And it belongs to the campus' resident douchebag, Elvin Plaud, one of the university student leaders of the New Progressive Party, the political denomination that wants assimilation to the United States. He's the son of Félix Plaud, top student advisor to the NPP during his college years, a chubby bro of color with some chin hair. Two peters in an oligarchy. That's when I decide to shut that voice down for good. The world does not need another voice like that. But I am shaking. I too want to obey and not be harmed.

I step out, throwing open the door. It's best to catch their leader's attention with my katana and hoping he knows what it means to unsheathe it only two inches and a half. He knows, oh, yes, he does. But his minions do not. So, I make sure they will remember all my friends' lives. With the first swing of my blade, down go three heads, four bodies I cut by the very middle, and twelve feetless and handless evil souls are released into the void. The rest stand aghast, far more frozen by my actions that whatever remains of their master's initial influence.

The general and I stand at a distance of maybe 35 feet, take or add a foot or two. I poise myself in the *gatoutsu* way and he does the cat stance, weaponless.

"Finally. Someone with dignity enough to face me. Or a measure of dignity whatsoever..." the terrorist says.

VI. The Threats

After September 11, things go awry on campus. Different factions take sides, as usually happens in times like these. The *Belongers* defend the United States' right to war, the *Macheteros* focus their efforts on different demonstrations favoring peace, and the *Conservatives* of course do nothing but fuel the fire. The student dorms are a powerful bastion of those who think freely, those who think like the *Macheteros* but fit in no group. Therefore, numerous attempts to terrorize their peace efforts are received by mail, with envelopes full of anthrax dust and dynamite packages that explode after opening. But at that time, I'm far more concerned with training and my coursework than with international affairs. My fencing and *iaido* classes are taking a toll on me. And then, I am part of a *capoeira/kokobalé* group, *La*

Comparsa, we are called. We're a bunch of Brazilian wannabes and Puerto Rican revivalists who really know our stuff, and at the time, I am learning the dreaded and exhausting art of dancing at the beat of the *rimbumbao*.

That's why I don't care when some *Macheteros* kick the shit out of Plaud years prior. He is a traitor, after all. Puerto Ricans who believe that Puerto Rico should be a state of the Union and actively fight for that cannot be deemed as anything but traitors. This is the truth in every narrative of the world. There is enough war in campus and I really don't need any more shit. I would pass by pro-war demonstrations, peace demonstrations, public demonstrations of apathy, and nothing could alter my system. Until the day I receive a strange envelope in my mail.

      Mr. Wyatt Ian González
      Ave. Universidad #4, 519
      Res. Torre del Norte
      San Juan, PR 00925
      BERRY IMPORTANCE!
      HANDLE WITH CAREFULLY!

There are messages like that in broken English all over the envelope. It is greasy on some parts, and it looks pretty much like the ones full of anthrax they had previously shown on TV, after Al-Qaeda leader Osama Bin-Laden brought the holy war on George's sorry ass. I put it against the light of the sun and shake it. There does not seem to be anything inside except paper. I open it.

The letter inside frightens even more than anthrax would. There's something about it, perhaps a menace, perchance an expectation.

We are ready to die! For the USA!
For the MOTHERcountry! This is War!
For the USA!

I feel bothered, for not only my privacy has been violated, but also my hard-fought peace. I tear it to pieces and keep my mind in my affairs.

The following weeks, the situation worsens. FOX and CNN encourage war, the rest of the news channels do not. Public opinion is engineered to be divided. And things in campus are not good. *Macheteros* and *Belongers* tear gas and molotov each other. Plaud is wounded more than once and, for the rest of the semester, he is forced to attend his classes accompanied by his bodyguards. However, things at the dorms remain calm. That's actually the purpose of international dorms. It's peaceful until more threats arrive.

One night, without any warning, it happens. The gunshots. Too close to sound like someone mugged and killed somebody in the neighborhood. No, this is now, this is here, too close to home to ignore any action. It does affect me because I can feel them approaching. So, I take my katana and start trembling, maybe out of fear, but also bloodlust.

VII. Bones, Thugs, and Harmony

One day, I spot a strange, yet recognizable figure some distance away. I am walking to the Natural Sciences building, and there's a guy with a diamond face. I'd recognize that face everywhere. It's the guy who robs me at gun point at my work, at the store that sells kinky stuff.

I hide because he's coming my way and wait for him to pass. Once he's ten or fifteen feet away, I follow. He goes several places in campus, delivering goods to different people from different departments. Even professors, janitors, and teaching assistants. At some point, he will have to go to the bathroom, and I'll be ready.

After a while, he crosses one of the campus streets and goes into the Education building, climbs the staircase, and finally, decides to stop at the second-floor restroom. I make sure no one is looking when I go in. As soon as I do, I lock the door behind me and walk to the urinals. He's there, pissing.

"I know who you are," I say.

He looks positively vulnerable, dick in hand.

"You robbed me several months ago."

He makes to turn, dick still in the air, to hit me, but I'm faster. I grab his arm and twist it behind his back, grab his hair with my free hand, and slam his face several times against the marble urinal.

"This is for me. And this... is for my friend."

I slam him more and more, until his body starts shaking uncontrollably, and then shakes no more.

I pull some paper towels and use them to grab his wallet from the back pocket of his jeans. "Gerard Matos," says his driver's license. Yet I find another ID that make leaves me seething. "Gerard Matos, New Progressive Party Youth."

I clean up and leave the restroom with the same confidence that he left my store when he robbed me.

VII. Sword on Malén St.

I have finished my training a week early and am looking for nothing in particular. *Iaido* is nice enough, but I also want to take ancient fencing and *kokobalé* classes. I have been going to the dojo for four years already.

Iaido is the Japanese art of wielding a *katana* at the speed of gods. Nothing quite like that, as I figure out later. It's just how to unsheathe and take out the sword at the last moment, right before impact. The last stance I am taught to me is the *batoujoutsu*, the sword of the wandering rebel. Stand in front, turn to your left, rotate your body this way, and hold your sheathed sword with your left hand, crossing your body horizontally like a bow. Then the rest is legwork.

Sensei Tomita tells me that I need not come back.

"There's nothing more that I can teach you," he starts. "And there's nothing more to learn about *iaido*, except to practice and keep that muscle memory."

At first, I feel bad, for humility propels you that way. Your master becomes your father, or a father you learn to appreciate, and after all that effort building bonds, it's quite difficult to cut those ties. And I still need more. So, I enroll in the fencing, *capoeira*, and *kokobalé* classes the next semester. The stances are different yet really empowering. Flashy and a little flamboyant, but the new moves for my repertoire are just what I need. Between the coupés and the swaying of the saber used to throw down your foe's weapon, I was amazed, and dashed by the triangularity of the fencing moves. Add to that *capoeira*'s *ginga*, the *aús*, and the *bananeiras*, and *kokobalé*'s circular wielding of the machete, and by mid-semester I'm ripped.

"You're ripped," Rosalina tells me one day. "I wanna get that ripped, too."

There's a shimmering quality to all those new movements and strikes that *iaido*, with all its geometry and perfect timing, does not possess.

Months after finishing the first semester of Fencing (EDFI 4221, 3 credits) I find myself walking down the sidewalk on Malén St., killing time by browsing the stores' windows. There are stores hidden in alleys, stores where no cops would go, for indeed Malén St. is no place for cops, or the faint-hearted. Some shops brim with exotic animals in small cages (tiny crocs, monkeys, bright blue salamanders, *grenouilles*, *guaraguaos*, birds of paradise...), stores with the most eccentric costumes and masks, antique shops, *botánicas* of all religions imaginable, magic kiosks (with the goriest ingredients: human shrunk heads, spider webs rolled up in balls, all types of moss and fungi, powdered cockroaches, rooster eyes and beaks...), drug dealing places, a very queer house at #455, and most interesting of all, at #455, an armory very famous for their antique valuables. There's a SPECIAL SALE sign in front and it's way too intriguing to pass.

As I come in, I wonder at the aisles full of medieval armor and morning stars, with shields adorned heraldically and bastard, vagrant swords that look like they were made for giants. There's even a sword that is also a whip, something that I had only seen in fighting videogames. It has Celtic inscriptions and carvings.

I move to a more Japanese part of the store and find classic nunchakus dating from before the Chinese immigration waves, iron made parasols and fans that spit poison needles from strategic points in their designs, and flags, tons of flags meant to be attached to samurai armor. The aisles are packed with these armors too, in red metal, blue, turquoise, silver, and gold. As I go deeper, I find what I am unwittingly looking for: the swords: *takemis*, *wakizashis*, and the *katanas*. I keep my pace, wondering what else I'll find, feeling the spookies crawling over my skin. Then I see it. A special Japanese sword with both sheath and handle made out of some kind of yellow-ochre-golden wood laced together with brilliant turquoise cords. With a sapphire on the tip of the handle, the cords on the sheath, which are also turquoise, the wood being the same strange yellow color, it is a masterpiece of destruction. "The Chirijiraden," reads the inscription, along with: 血を浴びる限り、その刃は決して鈍ることなく、忘れられることもない, which, more or less, means: *As long as you bathe in blood, your edge shall never dull nor be forgotten.* Tomita's Japanese has sure come in handy.

It may sound ridiculous, but the sword is placed in a part of the store where some beam of light falls exactly on it, as if it were the most divine artifact in this place. And indeed it is, for the Chirijiraden is perfection come from the hands of mankind. The perfect weight, the perfect balance between the two tips, the perfect edge, it is a convergence of things greater than human, more than mortal; it is a sword come from a time when things were made out of both necessity and beauty, born to be immortal and last forever. A thing born of the favor of *kamis*. I take it with my right hand, hold it horizontally in front of me, feeling as that perfection joins me in a converging bliss.

"That sword cannot be bought," says a voice from behind me.

I turn to look at the owner of that voice. It's a Japanese older-than-the-world woman. She has a very creased and wrinkled forehead, ears as pointy as human ears can be, and a long star-white hair.

"That's alright ma'am, I'm just window-shopping," I reply, returning the sword.

"Although, there is a way if you think you are fit. Tell you what, you can have the sword, if you do something for me. Come on, take it in your hands."

I grab it again with the same hand.

"Feel it," she says. "Close your eyes and feel him sing to you."

She takes a strange bow gun, one that has the power to cast five arrows at the same time, that much I can see. Then, after setting them all in place, she points it at me and shoots.

I don't know what to do at first, but then I remember my *iaido* classes. Mind is always quicker than anything else. Just take a look at how many things you can think in one second, how many people's faces you can see in two, how many smells you can remember in three... if you can only fathom all that and place it into one single thread of focused thought you may have the ability to unsheathe your weapon at the very last minute.

I see the arrows coming. That's a nice first step. All of them five moving towards me at the same time, at the same distance. Only one thing to do: to swipe them all off with just one thrust of my sword. It must be horizontal, so when they arrows are shot, I immediately switch my body to the *batoujoutsu* stance and unsheathe the Chirijiraden to the right, not quite knocking them with the blade, but more like creating a small wind void with the speed of the thrust, a wall of concrete air that stops them in their tracks. The old woman smiles with glee.

"Come with me. I want to show you something," she says, baring her teeth the way the monkey idols in the store's shrine do.

I follow her to the very end, at the back of the store, and she opens a door that leads to a very dark room. She turns on a light.

"See all those bodies with sets of four arrows in their chests? They came before you," she says without stopping to bare her teeth at me, and quite as-a-matter-of-factly. "I've a theory. I think you won it because you were only window-shopping. Not because you wanted it," and then she hands me a receipt, gives me a leather bag to put it in, and quickly leads me to the door.

"Don't come back again," she says, before slamming the store door in my face.

Freakiest day of my life.

VIII. Honor

It all happens in less than five minutes. I am behind the counter at the store. It is 7:00 p.m. It's an adult movie store. It used to sell condoms, dildos, and some other stuff for the satisfaction of fleshy pleasures, known or unknown. I am answering e-mails on the computer when the bell rings. We're talking about a store no more than 10.5' x 34', with a center aisle full of racks of DVDs. That leaves the front door, opening to the outside, in front of which lies an undefended and free path to the counter where I wait for the customer. The bell rings. It opens. It all happens in less than five minutes.

He comes like a storm, and points his gun at my temples, carefully brushing them with his .9mm.

"Give me all the money you've got here, man, and make it quick!"

I look at him. His face is naked, clean cut shaven, a nice impeccable white T-shirt tucked inside a pair of stonewashed indigo-gray jeans, butterscotch belt and shoes, and baby-blue-gray baseball cap, eyebrows plucked carefully and way too much. He sports a perfect square face, not that he has a square jaw, more like a diamond or a rhombus, the sides giving off an air of delicacy unseen until now in one of such character. And I say character because of what he does afterwards.

"Okay, just be at ease. I'll open the register for you."

"Make it quick, mutherfucker! You want me to put a hole in yo' head?"

"Alright. Alright. Just take it easy," I say trying to find the keys to the register. But they will not appear, and I am getting nervous.

When I finally open the cash register, there are only $77.00 in petty cash, from which he takes $17.00 between quarters, nickels, and dimes. His pockets are full of ringing coins, but he does not care. After that, he crosses around the counter and takes 167 DVDs ($2,750.00 in merchandise) between his right hand and the armpit, without even asking me for a paper bag.

"And you? Do you have anything?"

"I'm just a lowly student, man. And this is precisely why I never bring my wallet with me."

"Awright. Open that door, and if you call the police, I'll come back and shoot your head off."

And off he goes, leaving his threat lingering in the air like a hot and sweaty fart in an enclosed space. Off he goes, his pockets full of ringing coins, his gun in his left hand, and the 167 DVDs between his right armpit and right hand. As if nobody would question the fact that he has a gun in one hand and 167 DVDs in the other, not to mention the continuous ringing of those goddamn coins. I swear on that moment, on that very day, that I will allow certain humiliations never again. And I swear that if I see him again, I will cut his head off. Literally. It's a question of honor.

I remember news about a gang of robbers in the same area (probably this guy was one of them), who attack a friend of mine, and because he has no money, they hit him in the face several times with the butt of their guns, until they break parts of his skull, right below the right eye, and his nose. They leave him bleeding on the street and leave. I promise myself I am not going to let that happen to me, ever. It's a question of dignity and insomnia, the first because I value my life, the second because one must only carry the burdens that one can sleep with. When a life has to end, to keep on living is not only a waste of time and masochism, but an act of greed. So, I enroll in any self-defense class I can find. Fighting is my way to prove my worth. And I hope it always is.

Isentress

Pablo looks at the psychologist back and forth between his fingers and her face. She is a fine-looking young woman, who probably busted her ass in med school against a conclave of male breeders who probably couldn't take their eyes off her. He would ask her out, even though he's gay. Even though she's his shrink. His fingers are fine looking enclaves of touch, with a memory of bodies and a thousand memoirs that only resurface when he hits rock bottom. Like now.

"What's wrong, Pablo? You looked fine yesterday..."

"I'm... having suicidal thoughts."

"Are you able to identify why?"

"Nope."

"Everything ok at work?"

"I hate it, but it pays the bills."

"Can't you change?"

"Financial crisis, doc. Everyone's hanging on to their jobs for dear life. I'm no exception. Besides..." He pauses for air. She has green eyes. Gorgeous blades of grass. "Dad taught me that you're not supposed to like your job. You do it because you have to, and that's it."

"How do you feel about that?"

"It makes sense. It's kinda liberating in a way."

She looks at him with that quizzical expression he hates. Oh, boy, you are definitely a guinea pig. A rat. In. A. Lab. And the lab is your own screwed mindscape.

"What about your partner?"

"Vic's all right. He's good to me and I love him very much."

"How's the sex?"

"It's... difficult. When we met, we fell in love immediately. But sex with him is... tough."

"How come?"

"Well. Uhm. We're both tops. Or I was, anyway. I've forced myself to bottom for him."

"Do you not enjoy it?"

"I do. To a point. I guess?"

"And then?"

"And then... after a while, I just wanna die."

"Why?"

"I hate it. I hate having him inside of me. Having anything inside of me. I do it for him, but I hate it."

"Ok. Does he ever... what's the word you used?" She peruses through her notes. "Does he bottom for you like you bottom for him?"

"Nope. He's had anal surgery in the past. He can't bottom. He couldn't even if he wanted."

"I see. Why do you do it, then, if you don't like it? There are, after all, other ways of having sex without penetration…"

"Well, it seems that, in the gay world, there is no such thing as non-penetrative sex. It's not real. It's not… fulfilling?"

"And enduring receptive anal sex when you don't like it is fulfilling?"

There is a spiced flavor to the way she pronounces that last word. He doesn't say it right then, but he gets an erection he tries to hide by crossing his legs. He makes sure she doesn't notice. She notices.

"Are you taking your meds religiously?"

"Yes, ma'am."

The mere hint of HIV in the conversation softens his erection to oblivion. No wonder they call them shrinks, he thinks. She reminds him of his mom. Perhaps it's the smirk of knowing she has him locked in her prairie gaze. He wants to enter those eyes and graze in those fields. *What is wrong with me?* he thinks. *I have a beautiful man back home. The fuck is wrong with me?*

"What are you taking?"

"Truvada and Isentress."

"Huh…" she answers.

"Huh, what?"

"You know… Isentress is known from prompting suicide thoughts."

"Huh."

"Huh, what?" she asks playfully.

"So, the suicidal thoughts are not mine?"

"Don't you know that already?"

He looks at her, lost in the question, lost in the conversation, in those Mount of Olives eyes, those terrarium eyes, encased in layers and layers of transparent sheets of ice.

"I'll need to talk to your doctor. We need to see if you get better by changing your medication."

"Ok."

"Well, if that's it, then, I'll phone your doctor tomorrow and see you in two weeks, yes?"

"Yes," he says and makes for the exit.

"Wait, Pablo?"

"Yes, doctor?"

She uncrosses her legs and crosses them again, revealing a petulant disregard for panties that seems out of character enough to entice him.

"You shouldn't trap yourself in a relationship that doesn't satisfy you."

His erection rages again, forming a very visible tent, his kakis barely concealing the mushroom head and the teardrop of precum. *The fuck is wrong with my body, goddammit?!*

"Thanks," he says and leaves.

Outside the office, he stops at the restroom besides the elevators. He jacks off with no regard for his lack of lubricant. Cut penises need at least spit to achieve the ideal friction and prevent lacerations on the skin. He jerks and touches his own buttocks and even inserts a finger. He comes gloriously all over the urinal, cum even landing on his trousers and black T-shirt. Then, he cries, pants still down. A janitor enters and sees the crying man with pants and underwear at the ankles, member in hand.

"Yup," the janitor says. "She makes men crazy, that doc." And after a soft pat on the back, he leaves Pablo to pick his own pieces.

That afternoon, back at their house, Pablo showers while Leonard takes a crap. They trust each other that way. They are men, and they were childhood besties before becoming lovers. The bathroom is kind of small for such big war tanks of men. Leonard finishes, wipes his blond ass, flushes, and enters the shower.

"You should've sprayed some scent. It stinks."

"That's the protein, baby."

"Yeah," Pablo replies as he accepts Leonard's embrace from behind. Soon, the latter's erection probes against Pablo's magnificent ass.

"I've to talk to you," Pablo says.

"Uhm, sure, hon. What's on your mind?"

"I need a break."

"A break from what?"

"From the relationship."

There is silence, followed by the sound of towel-drying, the shelves opening and closing, the symphony of suitcases as they are unzipped and zipped again, and a finale of blasted doors. Leonard leaves.

Pablo lets him. He needs to cry again.

Back at the psych's office the week later, Pablo has made sure to wear the tightest underwear he has, as he undoubtedly wants absolute control and support of his meridian regions. While he waits at the reception area, a boy looks at him.

"Hey," the boy says.

"Hey, yourself, kiddo."

"Question: are you what you said you wanted to be when you grew up?"

"Wow. What a question. Why are you asking me this?"

"People are so sad here. They cry all the time. I watch them and want to hug them."

"Yes. I am what I wanted to be when I grew up," he lies. It's a beautiful lie. He always wanted to be a recognized writer, but when he saw the million writers in the world and the competition to be the best, to go for that Nobel Prize, which is the topmost one of the very few existent awards for writers, when he saw the backstabbing, the fierce bitchery, and even how some established writers pay off critics to trash the floor with the work of emerging authors, he quits. The final straw that breaks the camel's back is Bob Dylan's Nobel Prize of Literature. He loses all respect for it.

"What about you? A kid like you who seems so sure of life... what do you want to be when you grow up?"

"That's easy. I want to be a planet."

"Huh?"

"Pablo?" the doctor asks.

A woman comes out of the office. She has been crying a lot. She grabs the boy and leaves. The boy looks at Pablo and nods. A planet. As the doctor interviews him again, he ejaculates the same yadda yadda, yes, the pills, the Isentress is killing me, blah, blah, I can't take it anymore, please, help. What a joke. He thinks of a boy exiting the atmosphere in a rocket, then opening the lid of the pod, then exiting to float in outer space, in order to die, all the while exerting his wish upon the universe, a wish so powerful it becomes pure telekinesis, pulling mass around him, stars, satellites, and debris. He rotates in his death and becomes a warm center around which some life may revolve. That kid could have been Pablo, he thinks.

"So, he left?"

"It's not the first time. He does this when one of us needs space. Which is not too often, mind you."

"Do you trust he'll come back?"

"I don't know. We've known each other since forever, since we were kids, and honestly, I just don't know."

"Do you think he may be seeing another man."

"I doubt it."

"How come? Gay men can be so... free some times."

"Well, none of us is gay to begin with..."

She opens her eyes, clearly enticed by this new revelation.

"So... what are you?"

"Uhm... we're both straight men in a gay relationship."

"I'm sorry. This is a new one. Could you explain?"

"As I said, we had been buddies since we were kids. We have been the best of friends for a long time. Like brothers. Then, one day, I started feeling weak. It was a nervous disease brought by my HIV condition. I was at the brink of death, and he decided to move to my place and take care of me. I couldn't walk, as the condition attacked my sciatic nerve. I was bedridden and he took care of me. He made me better. He nourished me back to life itself. At a certain point, I started feeling sicker when he had to leave for work and surprised myself feeling like the happiest puppy when his owner comes back home. I don't know what this was. Maybe it was the fact that none of us had really been lucky with women, or perhaps it was the near-death experience. I think it was that. There's a point when you think life is ending and you find yourself unhappy and your body betrays you and your heart starts beating too fast when a certain person touches you in the most casual of ways, and then comes the time you have to throw all reason overboard and kiss that man that makes you that happy and who has taken upon himself to return you to the light, and I don't know... one day I confronted him. I told him that I found myself crying when he left for work and that my life was happy when he was around, and he told me he felt the same, that when he was at work, he felt a piece of him missing, and his heart being torn as if it were a magnet being ripped apart from his chest by the must unnatural of forces, his words, I swear, and then he asked me what I wanted to do about it, and

I stupidly replied with the same idiotic question, and we kissed. And the rest is history and adaptation."

She is flabbergasted at the story. Licking her pencil, she writes some notes the way someone would do in order to chart new, undiscovered territory.

"Wow."

"I'm sorry. I should probably have led with that."

"It's ok. I have never dealt with such a case. Have you tried contacting him?"

"We speak every night on the phone. I miss him."

"Is your space that worth the separation? I mean, I wonder whether the remedy is worse than your illness."

"I needed space. I needed to try and be with a woman. I have never really given myself that chance."

She gives him a quizzical look.

"You have his eyes," he states. "The same eyes," he says with some measure of due agony.

She stands up and gives him a card.

"I know what you need. This is my sister. She has an office downtown. Call her and make an appointment. You'll be glad you did."

Her office is located in a storage near the port part of the city. As he enters, he can see all sorts of dildos, whips, chains, chainmail, harnesses, buttplugs, and every little cunning toy of pleasurable torture the human mind can conceive.

"Come in, Pablo. Sarah told me about you."

"What did she say?"

"Only that you were coming," she replies in haste, to reassure him that no breach of doctor-patient privilege has been committed. They are twins, but their voices can be easily told apart. While Sarah's voice is sweet, unassuming, and soft, Cordelia's voice is adamant, tough, and bold. "Strip, please."

"Uhm, what?"

"I'm offering you the kind of therapy my sister can't. I'm Domina Cordelia. Strip and kneel before me. Now!"

Pablo does as he is instructed, revealing a raging hard-on that the woman caresses with the tip of her stilettos. She fits a harness around his massive pecs, all the way to his back, and around his pelvic area. The harness fits into a cockring of sorts, before intervening between the clash of his bulbous ass cheeks. She pulls at bit at the straps. The harness must be tight.

"Hands back," she says, and cuffs him.

"Uhm... I'm not really comfortable."

"That's what the safe word is for."

"So... what is the safe word?"

"Later," she replies as she blinds him with a fold.

"Ok."

"Choose a number higher than 50 and stand up."

"54."

"Ok. I'm gonna lash you 27 times on each cheek and you must count them individually. Like, I may be on my 14th lash on the left buttock and the 50th on the right one, and you must count this faithfully. If you lose count or you count more or less lashes by mistake, we reset and start again. I don't want to draw blood, so please, don't lose count. Also, if you piss yourself, I'll punish you. Do you understand?"

"Yes."

"Yes, Domina!"

"Yes, Domina."

He is made to kneel on rice while she flogs each buttock thrice. He counts out loud: "three left, fifteen right," and so on. She sits on a chair and beckons him to come closer. "Stick your tongue out," and flogs it lovingly. He squirms away, but she flogs his butt.

"Count!"

"Fourteen left, forty-four right!"

"Good. Now come forward."

He uses his knees as he can to propel himself forward without falling face first.

His tongue out, he proceeds until meeting a planet of burning and oozy flesh. It tastes of oatmeal. Instinctively, he pounds at it with his tongue.

"What. A. Rookie. Are you sure you're straight? You eat pussy like a faggot."

He flushes bright red, and she likes that. She grabs a medium size buttplug, smears it in her vagina and then slams it into his ass. He jumps and gasps for air, but she neutralizes his movements with a slap to the head. The tool is black and has a dog tail attached to it.

"Now, come forward! Again! And this time, lick it right! Put some minimum of emotion in it."

"I can't. My knees hurt!"

"They're not the only thing that'll hurt if you don't shut up and do as I say. Obey!"

This time, he circles his tongue, as he had been taught by his biology teacher when the group discussed recessive versus active genes. It turns out not just everyone can circle their tongues. He remembers a bisexual porn flick he used to watch with Leonard, about a straight couple training a gay man to have sex with them. The straight man would force the gay's head towards the woman's pussy and shout "Eat that pussy like a man!" Pablo thinks he can become a planet. That his telekinesis is his whatever skill he demonstrates here and now. That the mass, the stars, the satellites will be this woman who has taken so earnestly upon herself to teach him what only she can.

"Oh, you learn quick, you little faggot!"

She cums and squirts all over his face. He cums immediately, without actually touching himself.

"Oh, dear. That was good, wasn't it, Pablo? You may speak now."

"Yes, it was."

"Yes it was, what?"

"Yes, it was, Domina."

"Good. Now, since you came without my permission, you've got to pay for that. I want you to choose a number beyond 150."

"151."

"Ha. Cowardly lion. We may still make a man out of you. I will uncuff you and lead you to a bed. You need to be more comfortable to endure this."

He can't believe the tone of her words. There is a mix of emphasis, authority, and playfulness he can't pinpoint. It's just too new for him. Every time he thinks he understands what's going on, she unnerves him with a new game. After placing him lovingly on the bed, the way you would a puppy or kitty, and removing his blind fold, she orders him to assume a fetal position, and solidly straps him there. There's no changing or shifting position the way he's bound.

"I'll be back in a minute or two. I'm looking for something special."

When she returns with a 9" x 5" black rubber dildo, he opens his eyes and starts crying. He tries to move, but he can only tremble all over. His body is betraying him again.

"It's ok. I am here for two purposes, Pablo, and it's imperative that you know. First, I'm here as a substitute for a woman. I mean, I'm a woman, but I'm here replacing the one you never had the chance to have sex with. Two: I'm here to open the hell out of that ass, so you can go back to that delicious boyfriend of yours and he can fuck the piss out of you. Comfortably. Do you understand? Now, you chose the number 151. I was going to impale this dildo into you the number of times you chose. But since you've been such a coward faggot, I will impale you 151 times 151 with this dildo. Meaning, 22,801 times. And you'll count them for me. The same rules apply as with the flogging. If you forget the count, we have to start again. Say you understand."

"I understand, Domina."

"Say you're my little bitch and that you want this huge dick up your ass."

"I'm your little bitch, Domina. And I want your huge dick up my ass."

"Let's start, then!" she giggles in excitement.

She places a red gag on his mouth and smears a very thick white goo on the dildo and around and inside his anus. Then, she pushes. His scream is muffled. He soon finds out how much a simple red ball in the mouth can dampen his pleas for release. One. To the very base. He screams, nevertheless. One! She withdraws entirely and he is left trembling. He wants to piss desperately. And crap. But he has been ordered to hold his own. Here she comes again. Two! Good puppy! She kisses his anus after withdrawing. Her tongue circles the ring muscle and then enters. He moans in terrible pain and pleasure. She opens his legs a bit and reaches for his hardened cock, sucking enough to send him over the edge without making him cum. The next twenty-five thrusts come as a machine gun assault. Twenty-seven! He cries. His body is a building somewhere along the San Andreas Fault. She is a sort of earthquake, and her dildo is a force of nature. Ten more thrusts, and he's already attempting to remember the number. Thirty-five!

"Yes, you're doing great!"

She decides to attach her dildo to a fucking machine and send the rest in one go. He doesn't miss a single blow count. When she withdraws, he faints.

"What's up, baby? Are you ok?" she asks.

He opens his eyes as the alcohol wakes him up.

"What happened?"

"You fainted, but you took it like a hero."

"What happens now?"

He is naked, in a more comfortable position but still tied to bed.

"Now, I make you cum with the dildo up your ass."

She climbs on top of him and rides his erection. It doesn't take him more than five minutes to empty. She curses and then squirts all over his face, returning his own cum to him along with her own gushing fluid, which is a mix of mostly urine and her natural lubricant. There is no real name for it. A Puerto Rican lesbian poet calls it *fluvis* whereas some Micronesian tribes call it *momola*. It's so rare it doesn't have a universal name. He knows he can't speak of this. No one would believe him anyway.

After ejaculating, she unstraps him and gives him an appointment for the following week.

"If you miss our appointment, I'll go find you at work and humiliate you in front of all your colleagues. You don't want that. Be sharp."

"Yes, Domina."

The next appointment, he arrives in a white T-shirt and jeans. She orders him to undress. He does this more comfortably and with more ease than the previous week.

"Today, I won't punish you. I'll teach you. You've been a good boy and you deserve a treat. You see that traffic cone over there? Bring it here."

He does as instructed. She places it firmly on the ground and smears the same white fluid she had used on him before. She places a bit inside his anus.

"Now, I want you to squat there, barely touching the tip of the cone with your ass. I don't want you to insert it just yet. Are we clear?"

"Yes, Domina."

"Yes, Domina," she replies in such a mocking and loving voice that he smiles. "You're such a cute little dog. I think I may fall for you. Now, we can't have that, can we?"

She leaves him squatting there. Five minutes later, she brings several federal caselaw digests within a small red cart, and a small and strange metal contraption with a lock. She grabs his balls and penis and places everything within the device. She shuts the lock.

"What is that?"

"Did I give you permission to speak, dog?! Do you want some flogging?!"

"I'm sorry, Domina. It won't happen again."

"Good dog. Now shut up and hold this for me." She tosses one of the federal volumes for him to grab without falling or inserting the cone in his ass. One tome, two tomes, a tower of sixteen tomes.

"Remember. Do not let the cone rape you or I'll have to rape you with it. I'll go watch my Latin telenovela. You stay here and strengthen those muscles."

She will return every once in a while, presumably during commercials, to check on him. He endures. Barely, but he does. In the end, she places five more tomes on top of the tower and tells him to relax his anus and let it happen. When he does, he can't believe how easy it is to be penetrated by such a huge object. And how pleasurable it is against his prostate.

"You like that, don't you, little faggot?"

"I love it, Domina."

"Good. I want you to continue until you come."

"But, Domina... how can I come if my penis is caged?"

"Good question. I don't know. Find out. I'll leave you to it. Think about that wonderful boyfriend you have. Invoke his presence and feel him fucking the hell out of you. Feel it and enjoy it. I'll turn off the lights to aid with the visualization. Good luck!"

Three weeks after the appointment, Pablo calls Leonard. He leaves a message.

"I miss you too much. And I need you back in my life. Come back, please."

Two hours later, they are together in bed. Leonard is surprised by Pablo's willingness to give up his ass and enjoy it. Leonard cums 7 times inside his lover's anus.

"What brought this change?" he asks Pablo.

"You'll meet her soon," he says, and takes his Isentress nightly medication. The doctor has told him he can't change the drug for another. He has decided to bear with the suicidal thoughts until he can. "Her name's Cordelia, and you'll just love her."

Old Man Nereus

I

> *I could just drift, he thought, and sleep and put a bight of line around my toe to wake me.*
> *But today is eighty-five days and I should fish the day well.*
>
> *Just then, watching his lines, he saw one...*
> **Ernest Hemmingway (*The Old Man and the Sea*)**

I climb down the rocks, hidden mostly by sea grape bushes, remembering many useless things about the species. *Coccoloba uvifera*, only large-leafed species usable for bonsai purposes, for the leaves can be shrunk; eat its berries only when they are very ripe red, or else you might get a nasty case of instant diarrhea... My right foot slips a little and I fall on my butt, seating on a rock. *This is stupid.* I could log on Manhunt or Adam4adam and find me a host of big assed, large-cocked men to play with. I don't need to go cruising in the most unreliable part of San Juan. Yet, I push onward through the trees and shrubs, the scarce sand on the rocks, and all the used needles, soda cans, and general rubbish.

I step on the beach and walk past the remaining trees until I find a trail made by countless men over the ages. The sand here is hard, almost solid, the grains heated together by the sun into a glass quality. As I keep walking, I wonder how many men have walked this path before me, how many Spaniards in search of *cimarrones*, how many Arawak men seeking secluded sex with other men. I finally step out of the greenery and spot a disheveled structure a few paces from me. As I get closer, it starts to look like a house made of debris that the sea coughed up in a tantrum of storms. Where there's a structure, there must be people, so I take my clothes off, put them in my backpack, and walk naked.

The hut has several divisions made with rotten cloth, rope, and bamboo poles. I can identify at least three open rooms, with several weathered mattresses lying around. A kid no older than 22 smokes hashish from a homemade pipe. He is in his loose white jockeys, his young prick coming out of the leg seams. An old, black-bearded man with several golden earrings plays with his dick underneath his black briefs. Though their skins have been severely burned by time, weather, and sun, even in their equally bronzed skin tone they look unrelated. I walk by and I wonder at all the possible names that come to my mind describing that house: hut, structure, cabin, *bohío*, shithole, dollhouse, stash... they pay no attention to me at all, and I move onward.

When I'm some meters away from the hut I feel some movement behind me. The old man is pissing on the sand. His cock is long and pencil-like. It looks like a lump of flesh or molding clay that some trickster god gave away as alms for a poor bastard. He pisses hard and doesn't care when I look intently and rub myself. When he finishes, he bids me closer with his hand.

"Oi, come 'ere!"

"Are you talking to me, sir?"

"Of course. Come to my hut, son!"

I slowly rev my way back to his house. He takes his black briefs off and goes into the structure first.

I approach and notice that the kid is tripping hard, his eyes rolled up high, revealing only the whites. The old man is sucking him off.

"Do you want some? He's ripe for the taking."

I'm not sure what to say when the old man grunts a noncommittal "suit, yourself," rolls the kid over and penetrates him. My dick grows hard almost immediately.

"Come 'ere, fuck him. Let me look at you while you fuck my grandson."

"Is he really your grandkid?"

"Close enough."

The old man rolls away but stays close to ply open the kid's ass with his hands. I insert my hard cock inside and it feels sandy. But I fuck it relentlessly all the same.

"Give it to him, come on. Cum inside."

I erupt in ropes spraying the kid's guts with my seed. The old man then pushes in and fucks him until he comes too. Then, he pisses again. Long streams of yellow and pungent liquid on the dreaming boy, who simply doesn't want to wake up.

"Uhm… is he going to be ok?"

"Sure. No problem at all. Listen, son, drugs are like that. They make you high and then they don't break hold of you until they do. It's as simple as that. Now scram! I've got some fish to catch."

I stay for a while, watching from a distance as the old man, still naked and evenly tanned, breaks into his fishing activity. He improvises a rod from a curved sea grape branch (there are only sea grapes on this beach) and some rope thread and tosses it into the calm sea. There are no waves in this beach.

Half an hour later, the kid wakes up, finds himself naked and drowsily makes a hole in the sand. He expels and urinates there. When he smells urine on himself, he throws a fit at the old man.

"You old coot bastard. Pissing on me again? You fucker! I should kill you, old man!"

The granddad just laughs hard, his golden teeth glinting in the sunlight. The kid goes into the sea, presumably to wash. On his way to the water, the old man grabs his ass and cock.

"Leave me alone!"

"Oh, come on! You know you like it, you little pervert!"

The kid opens his ass with his hands and moons at the old man.

"Yummy!"

While the kid swims, the old man beckons me closer again.

"He likes it, you know. Waking up with the white inside. You know what I mean?"

"Yes," is the only thing I can say to this man who has adopted me as his sexual confidant.

"It seems there aren't fishes around. Wanna go inside the hut?"

"Sure," I reply, fascinated at what treasures could be found there.

The door to the hut is an improvised gate made with corroded latticework that someone must have dumped on the beach, pulled tight with thin white rope and fastened with small mounds of the very sand. The walls are plastered with pictures of women in underwear from Macy's and

JCPenney catalogs. There are also pictures of women in bikini from the pinup section of the local newspaper.

"Let me see that ass."

I turn over to show him my naked butt.

"Hold on. Put this on."

He gives me brand new, black lace thong panties. Opened at the crotch.

"Really? Do you want me to put this on?"

"Come on. I wanna see that white boy ass in those panties."

I put them on while he says "slowly, that's it, *mijo*." He strokes his cock.

"Come 'ere. Put it in yo' mouth."

I don't think I can, thinking of microbes, old beggars, and their stench. His cock is surprisingly clean and while I suckle the glans, he pulls my head further into his pubes with one hand and traces circles around my lace-thonged hole. He inserts a finger.

The grandson arrives and goes inside his makeshift room, picks another pair, red and green Christmas novelty panties, to be exact, that some tourist must have left on the beach, puts them on, and presents his cock to my face. He pisses and I am barely able to close my eyes.

"That's it. Piss hard, son. You. Suck him off. I'm gonna fuck me those panties."

I feel the old man caress my butt and push through. It hurts. I make to jump but they hold me fast. And then I lose it. In my mind, as my most vulnerable land of flesh is invaded, I actually welcome the microbes, the fungi, and the bacteria. The viruses I fear. He grunts and I feel him fill me up inside. The kid takes his cue and fills my mouth with his seed. He doesn't let go until I swallow.

"Ok, party's over. You run along now."

And he doesn't even ask me to give him back his panties.

II

Then rose from sea to sky the wild farewell—Then shriek'd the timid, and stood still the brave,— Then some leap'd overboard with fearful yell, As eager to anticipate their grave.
Lord Byron ("Don Juan")

I wait several weeks before going back. There's something about that beach, about being naked among rubbish, kissed by the sun and the breeze, and the salt of the water. There's something in the line of inspiring lust in those who see me walk with an erection obscenely dangling from side to side. As I climb down from the city atop the hill to the secluded beach, I think of useless things, like how come one grain of salt in a bottle of water does not affect its taste, and on the nature of invertebrates and how can anyone move without the support of bones.

I make my way past the *Coccoloba* shrubbery. The two men are arguing loudly in front of their hut.

"I didn't rob you!"

"No? Look at this! Look at this mess! Someone came in here! The only mutherfucker living with me is you!"

"Old man, I swear! Nereus, I swear, I didn't take anything!"

"Scoot, boy! I don't wanna see you anymore."

"Fuck you, grandpa. FUCK YOU!"

The boy leaves in his white jockeys, a pair of jeans, and a shirt hanging from his right shoulder.

"The fuck are you looking at, bitch?" he asks as he passes me.

He sits under a sea grape, rolls a blunt, and smokes. He takes off his briefs and lies on the sand, soaking in the sun. I turn to Nereus.

"Excuse me. Would you happen to have a cigarette?" I ask just to make conversation, realizing soon and too late just how idiotic I sound.

"Do I look like I have a cigarette, son? Do you wanna smoke this one, son? Eh, son?"

He grabs his crotch in a vulgar way and goes inside the only room left in his ransacked hut. Things start to fly out the door, mixed with insults to none in particular and much swearing. I make to leave when he stops me.

"You. Come 'ere."

He takes off his black briefs.

"Suck me off. Come on, I need it."

I look into his eyes and see desperation, but also loneliness. Deep ocean trenches that not even the glinting of his teeth under the sun can illuminate. He is hard and waiting for me. I take off my shorts and reveal the crotch-less black lace thong panties. When I take his erection in my mouth he bursts in piss. It tastes like raw vinegar. Or pure methylene. I drink every single drop, and when he erupts again, this time with his seed, I swallow it all and say thanks.

"You better go now, son. Things are gonna get ugly here."

I leave almost immediately. When I'm about to enter the greenery to climb the rocks and exit the beach, just before, I see a hint of light reflected. Steel. A makeshift shank in his right hand. Not his teeth.

III

Grampa walked up and slapped Tom on the chest, and his eyes grinned with affection and pride.
"How are ya, Tommy?"
"O.K.," said Tom. "How ya keepin' yaself?"
"Full a piss an' vinegar," said Grampa.
John Steinbeck (*The Grapes of Wrath*)

I go back three days later. I need to see the old man, make sure he didn't do anything stupid against the boy. I find the hut has grown bigger. Another debris-made room has been annexed. As I walk by, the boy says hi from behind his hashish pipe. His eyes roll up and go white. Another man leaves the room. He is fully clothed.

"So, no problem, then? I can stay here?"

"Sure," the kid says.

The old man is nowhere to be seen. I wait for the new guy to leave, and then go inside what used to be Nereus' room. There are no longer pictures of women in lingerie, or the *Primera Hora* pin girls. Two mattresses are laid wildly on the sand floor.

I talk to the boy.

"Where's Nereus?"

"Who's Nereus?" he asks.

"Your grandfather. The old man with the golden teeth. Where is he?"

He blows some opiate smoke. Blue with a gray quality. He points to the sea.

"Somewhere over there. He went back home."

And then he rolls over and falls asleep. I get hard immediately. I pull down his jockeys and penetrate him. No lube, no spit, no compassion. *If you killed the old man, there's no restraint.* I fuck him for

161

hours, until I fill him up. Then, while still inside, I take a piss. In his drug dream, he doesn't even moan. There's no pain. So, I fuck him again, even harder than the first time. And again I cum. I take his clothes with me. Just for dumb sake: Christmas panties, white jockeys, jeans, red t-shirt, everything goes into my backpack. And I leave.

As I trace my way back to leave the beach, I see glints of gold and silver. Better go now. Old man Nereus is coming.

Tarot for Writers

I

He places the green wrapped bundle at the side of the night table. The reading is about to begin, and I look as he takes the cards, shuffling them as I shuffle my way into those dark olive eyes, almost as if pulling me in. I am nailed to the spot by those eyes and the invisible weight they levy on me, by force of will or some higher nature, or a higher intelligence. For one thing, those eyes are like green-black fire, smoldering my own, and I can resist only by closing mine.

"Your turn to shuffle the cards. Mind you, pay no mind to the order in which you do."

Startled to have my mind back, I sit and try to relax. I take the cards and do the best I can to clear my mind, especially from doubts. What have I got to lose, after all? But then, I think about writing, about finishing the next novel I am due next month, and all the pressure of being a writer from the confines of my home, like how the hell am I going to pay the rent during the covid world-wide quarantine, the way I'm getting a little bit fat despite the fact that I'm thinner than a bamboo stick... and then, the higher things, like am I writing what I'm supposed to, or am I a good writer, am I an impostor, and then, where's the love of my life... When I'm done, I take a deep breath and look around me. His bedroom is tidy, that much I can say. His very few belongings are arranged in impeccable *feng shui*. More specifically, the curious wire-made table with intricate Celtic knots right in front of the window, a night table to its right, two wooden chairs on which we currently sit, his lustrous black satin bed positioned right beside the wall so it won't hinder the energy coming from the window, and a fish tank with no fish at all, but a lot of stunning crystals of all possible colors grown with sea salt.

"When you finish shuffling, part the cards in three groups and wait."

I feel compelled to ask.

"Umm, Xavier, how do you know the meaning of those cards?

"I'm a nerd who's studied them all his life."

"Really? Yeah, well, of course, I know. But... See, what I really want to know is how come all things in life can be read in the Tarot? I mean, life is made up of too many things, and my best guess is that a set of 78 cards cannot represent it all."

"Well, things that are too trivial do not echo in the spread. As for what's really important, one card can have more than one meaning. It also has significance in regard to the cards surrounding it."

He flips the first card. The Fool.

"This is you, Lorenzo, not a real fool, but a person willing to brave social distancing and quarantine measures for enlightenment, inspiration, or perhaps a hero in a quest, that or a very stupid person who's about to commit the mistake of his life. What would it be? Let's see."

He flips the card on top of the next group.

"Ah, the Queen of Cups upside down. Either your mother or a very powerful woman still has the reigns over your life, or we can go back to your first card and say that you're in desperate need for inspiration. As for the final card... There! The Moon. I take it you are an artist, a writer perhaps?"

When he sees how astounded I am, he grabs one more card from the middle cluster, the group for easy responses. It's the Two of Swords.

"I'm sorry, but right now, I don't know what this card means. Let's take another one."

He flips a final card from the left group. The Two of Pentacles.

"Misery. That or an overpowering, overwhelming, and overkill success."

He looks at me and all I can do is stare at the floor to avoid those unmerciful, yet forgiving and pleasant eyes.

"I take it is a writer's block, isn't it?"

That day, Antonio's adrenaline at almost breaking curfew siphons his energy and air as he runs back home. He sits down and tries to write. Everything is against him that day, the same way everything that's against him every time he tries to write. *The writer's curse,* he thinks. Whether it's a radio in the neighborhood with some full throttle reggaeton, or the need to go to the bathroom, or the sudden whim of eating a devil's food and vanilla cake, there's always something better to do than write. And he must fight those urges. He develops a kind of strict discipline, a daily rhythm that helps him organize his telework tasks and domestic chores, and which also comes in the form of outlines. He's got outlines for speeches that he will never give at universities, of inspiring novels that he may never get to write, even if he survives the pandemic... he's even got outlines of the points he needs to discuss with his mother next time she calls. *Oh, my God, I'm such a control freak*, he will tease himself.

His lover, Damien, stops at the door to their room.

"Are you ever gonna have supper?"

"Not now. I've got to write," Antonio replies without even glancing back, for he's just an ant in this world, gazing upon the open window, looking for words that form chains, and chains that form strings, and strings that pave and paint entire worlds that need to exit from deep within him, or he will explode. Sometimes he feels like a time bomb, waiting for the right circumstances to birth another Big Bang, a black hole, or a white one. Always looking for something to absorb and transform into a good setting, an unforgettable character, a story made with the substance of the memorable.

"Working? Again?"

Antonio turns to Damien and has the most beautiful, lost expression on his face, but does not look at his lover. Instead, his eyes rest on some imaginary object right through Damien.

"I think I may have a first sentence."

"Oh, yeah...? Supper must be, then. Proper supper, husband and husband together at the table, do you know what I'm talking about?"

"Can't. Must work."

"Ok. Listen. I know you need to finish that book by the end of the month, but this is ridiculous. I barely see you at all, and we're together in a fucking quarantine!"

Antonio gives him the fiercest, most feral glance as Damien steps back into the shadows of the stairs, making the usual thumping noises as he climbs down, finally ending it with kitchen clatter. He looks at one of the books on the shelf to the right of a strange bundle wrapped in green cloth. Virginia Woolf's *Mrs. Dalloway*. *Gina, Gina, what would you do in my shoes?*

I think I may have a first sentence... He writes on his laptop:
>*He wakes up, trembling with emotion. His first words are: "I'm going to do something extraordinary today!".*

He wakes up, trembling with emotion. His first words are: "I'm going to do something extraordinary today!" In the background, his alarm radio goes off on The Weeknd's "Blinding Lights." What an affirmation! Michael dances to the thought of a limitless life and feels content because he is still safe, untouched by the invisible virus everyone thinks is airborne. He senses that he can reach to the clouds with his bare arms and steal an idea in the palm of his hand. The morning has a soft light, unblinding to his eyes; the quiet murmur of the river and the city locked down by the worldwide emergency low in his ears, almost caressing. He has woken with a deep love for all living things and decides he's indebted. Today is about repaying, about gratitude for the life given. But how can you do that from home?

Still, there's something odd about this abrupt awakening and the statement that follows. He remembers having read somewhere that the moments before a catastrophe are the most perfect in the lives of those who endure it. The back of Michael's neck burns, as if someone were watching him. He turns several times, but of course there's no one there, as he's locked down inside his house. So, he resumes his exercise of meditating, looking for something extraordinary to do today. Shall he write an email to an old friend, any of those with whom he was tight before Hurricane María? He decides against it. It's been three or four years, for instance, since he last talked to Sara, his best friend, or Laura, his colleague from his old job. He has never had many friends, so he discards the idea. Writing after such a long time incommunicado... how do you do that? How do you reconnect with someone whom, at some point in your life, you decided was not worth the energy of staying in touch with? People call it "drifting away," as if life itself were an intelligent creature who could actually extend her invisible and magic claws from the abyss to pull people apart in the concrete world. Something else, then. He thinks back to the picture album he went through the day before, gazing right there upon his adolescence, his graduation from Med School, and his first marriage. *Damn, you were certainly happy in those days!* Why wasn't he anymore? He keeps thinking on what to do, in that horrible way in which leisure time becomes so vast and all-engulfing that all books promise the same story, all movies have the same dialogues, all series feature a musical episode, and all songs are sung with the same disgusting melisma. And you need to find something to do to justify being alive. *Think! What is the one thing that you've never done in your life that you can actually do in quarantine?*

Michael closes his eyes and goes back to two weeks before, when he went to the market. There are kiosks of all kinds, one for every single vulgar and earthy taste. They have the funniest names, like I Can, You Can't Botanic, Mrs. Batida, El Pulpito Seafood, The Dancing Cangrejero... Some people are already starting to wear masks and gloves. Most, however, are barehanded and baremouthed. Some old lady stops her walker mid-corridor to cough her life out, barely covering her snout with her left elbow while supporting herself on the walker with her free hand. Then, she continues walking slowly, until she exits the market. He follows her out into the street.

"No! Stop!"

She's about to be hit by a midnight blue Honda Civic '96. He runs and pulls her back in time to save her life. She falls on top of him, and for a minute, their eyes connect, and time stops. Then, he gradually notices as her face disfigures into the muscular spams that will make cough possible. He is not able to shield himself before her rain of spit and germs falls on his face. Someone helps her up, and then him, and he rushes to the restroom inside the market to wash his face and mouth, all the while reminding himself not to swallow. Although, he's not shallow as to do good stuff for the sake of praise, it stings him that his one heroic act of saving a life goes unnoticed because he has to wash her germs off his face. When he looks up at the mirror, a homeless man is taking a leak in one of the urinals, pants down the ankle, his scrawny ass so emaciated that his swollen hole will be left open for the world to see even if he tries to clench what little buttocks life has left him with. The bum leans his forehead to the wall and starts coughing. *What if the Wuhan plague is here already?* The thought assaults Michael all the way out of the bathroom and to the market. *Don't call it Wuhan plague, even if it's true*, his politically correct side interferes.

To get his mind off it, he buys a *batida* of banana, papaya, vanilla, and brown sugar. He sits down at one of the tables and looks around. Is there anything extraordinary left to do today that will take this demonic boredom away?

Lorenzo goes back home. He starts writing at 1:37 p.m. The alarm radio plays The Weeknd's "Blinding Lights", and there's that green wrapped bundle. After the first sentence, words become a fluid he pours into his computer. He is in the zone, a godly architect building a world with words in a piece of humankind's most ancient technology, the tale. He's doing the Dance of Yahweh, the Creator, his hands going up in the air and then turning back down with fury, as a flurry of fingers makes descriptions, dialogues, internal monologues, streams of consciousness invented by William James, and not Virginia Woolf... Seven days later, when the novel is finished, and he gazes at the screen of his laptop in bewildered amazement and pure exhaustion, he notices that he didn't really write. He channeled. Like some force greater than everything not just whispers the story in his ears, but also imbues him with the emotional energy to write it. The wanting needs to do it. The wanting urges him to do it. By the time he is able to pick himself from the floor, his body is that of a frail old lady trying to cross a street, his head that of a young man trying to save her from being hit by a car. He is undeniably tired. So, he goes to sleep. After all, there's not much to be done during quarantine. Meanwhile, in the realm of written worlds, another one writes on his laptop.

Antonio rejects every single one of Damien's attempts to make him eat. He's trying to concentrate, and each word is in single line waiting for him to grab them down from style heaven. ADD is kicking in and he's out of Adderalls. He closes the door to his office room and locks himself in. But the ideas are gone. Or the will to transform them. Some other time, he would just go out to the park and walk, maybe cruise for some gay sex in the restrooms, or do some people-watching. But in the middle of the worldwide lockdown to try and flatten the curve of infection, that's not even an alternative. It's still several hours till curfew, so maybe he can feign going to the market, which is one of the rather few reasons the authorities are allowing people out for without arresting them. He hangs a mask around his neck instead of putting it on, takes a pair of latex gloves, and goes past the door without even bothering to say "See you later" to Damien or tell him where he's going. Desperation for purpose kicks in and overrides him, even if it means going out to danger without saying a goodbye to his most beloved in full knowledge that he could very well not come back.

He visits the market and sits opposite to a very handsome man without mask or gloves who looks like he's in his mid-thirties. He's drinking a milkshake, probably from the Mrs. Batida kiosk. Suddenly, the stranger looks at him. For a moment, their eyes click, and they both engage in a dream of what a future together would look like. It's a fleeting thing that people often do unconsciously when they lock eyes with strangers. Things he has never thought in his life come to mind, for instance, how much of a life can you imagine with a stranger, how much of yourself do you project into the stranger as a character in your future love life, or how come writing about these weird connections make you feel like they can happen, even if they can't. Their gazes unlock after Antonio lowers his eyes. *I'm not the weak one*, he thinks. *You are.* He stands up abruptly, nods at the stranger, and leaves.

Back home, he sees some neighbors going through the ritual everyone's talking about on Twitter, Facebook, and international news. Local news are slow on the uptake, and that is often the problem with pandemics. His neighbor from two houses to the right, Frank, greets him bare-assed as he finishes removing his clothes before going inside his home. He has removed everything, and his cock is hanging in the air as he quickly sprays some of that 50% water / 50% alcohol solution that they say kills the coronavirus. He turns his hairy ass to Antonio before spraying each inorganic item of this grocery list with the same solution. *We should probably start doing the same shit*, Antonio thinks.

As he goes back in, ideas flow back, a stammering, unending stream of stories, or possibilities, waiting to be put on paper. He heads straight into his office room and locks the door again, leaving a frustrated and sad Damien gawking behind. He doesn't get out of the room until the novel is finished. Seven days later.

Michael stares at the stranger staring back at him. Their eyes lock, and for a minute, the thought of a life together with this stranger overrides his mind. In his imagination, they meet here and, guided by a force they can't identify, they lock themselves in a cubicle in the restroom and make love in silence and sobs. Then, a few months later, they get married, but they never tell their friends the real story of how they met cruising in a dirty public restroom. Just before the stranger withdraws the imposition of his eyes upon his, he knows he'd have been beaten at this staring game. He's weak from the contest of wills. The stranger nods at him and he curtsies back with his eyes. Then the stranger leaves, and a hungry and dirty homeless man sits in his place, showing off his hunger all over the place with his thin, emaciated persona. He looks tired, famished, and miserable. It's so heartrending, that Michael stands up, goes to La Bellaca Criolla Café, and buys him some *arepas, arroz con habichuelas,* and a Coca-Cola. He leaves before the hobo can thank him. Withdrawing to a dark aisle he's never seen before, he spots, at the farthest left, a strange kiosk with a big sign rimmed in intermittent neon, that reads:

Want to know your doom?
TAROT READINGS
at Mr. X

For starters, this kiosk is strikingly different from the rest, not just because of the neon lights, but also due to its Old-World vibe, the bright velvety colors of the drapes that border the window, or the many intermittent Christmas lights that adorn the entrance. Or maybe it's the red-tailed hawk skull hanging from the door. Inside, it's also brighter and far cleaner than the other kiosks. A cockroach coming from the stairs stops dead at the entrance, and goes back the way it came from, as if uninterested or terrified. Also inside, the fine incense gives off its aroma, and from its many notes, it can be appreciated that it's not the garden variety that can be bought at the supermarket, but one made by plain old fashioned, proud human hands who have the will and emotion to make it.

Hmmm. I've never gone to a place like this. He decides to check it out.

> *Hmmm. I've never gone to a place like this. He decides to check it out.*
>
> It reads that way in Lorenzo's novel. Chapter seven, page 156, paragraph two:
>> He goes inside Mr. X's. There's a man behind the counter. He's easy to the eyes in a very strange, almost terrible way, especially when he locks his dark-olive green eyes with the eyes of an unwary passerby. Modern haircut, raven black, disorganized, as if

he had more important things to do than take care of his personal grooming. His chin's shaved, though.

"Excuse me. How much for a consultation?"

"It depends. Are you braced to listen?"

"Why... of course. If not, I wouldn't have come here in the first place."

"Good answer. Everyone always says the same thing, even if they find themselves wildly wondering why in hell they paid a handsome man like myself to read them their fortunes. Come with me."

They settle at the back of the kiosk, which suddenly looks even more spacious, if such a thing is possible. A green cloth lay on the table with intricate Celtic knots. He passes the deck to Michael.

"My name's Xavier. Shuffle the cards. Mind you, pay no attention to the order in which you do."

Michael does as instructed. When he's ready, he casts a glance at the Tarot master.

"Now, part them in three groups."

Michael does, and immediately, the hand that rocks the future starts flipping cards. The Hanged Man, the Chariot upside down, and Death. *A slowly, but steady walk towards Death, that ends today.* Xavier looks at his client with careful, cold, and calculating eyes.

"Are you sure you want to be told what is yours by right to know?"

"Definitely."

"Very well, today is the last day of your life."

After a long, muted space of time that lasts no more than mere minutes, Xavier breaks the silence.

"Since you are dying today, and henceforth, there's no more to say, consider this reading on the house. Have a lovely afternoon, while you can."

"No, wait. You can't leave me like that. Please."

"Very well, pick one more card."

It's the Two of Swords. A woman in a white tunic sits in front of a waterfront with her eyes bound by a white cloth and holds two swords while her arms cross over her chest, like she's a dead body in a coffin. The Tarot master seems confused, and stares at the card for a long time.

"I've never gotten along with this card. It doesn't matter how much I study it, it always seems to flutter away from my understanding. Very well, I don't need another card to tell you what I must. Right now, you should think of what would make you happy. Hell, you should be thinking of having the most wonderful day you can. After all, it is your last. Also, have you ever locked eyes with someone, a stranger, and felt that you could be happy with that person, and imagined an entire life together?

"Yes, I have," Michael is compelled to answer.

"Well, there's that. Have a lovely afternoon."

With that, Michael comes back to the aisle, back to the spaces that are real, back to the world that awaits. Blinking his eyes does no good, the confusion is still there, but the kiosk is nowhere to be found. Everything Xavier told him he remembers as if he'd just woken up from a pleasant, yet admonitory dream. He thinks of the last time he had a smile on his face. It was the day he was told he was going to be a father. It was a week before; his wife ran away from him, had the baby in a country too far away and sent him a note and a post card. *Don't follow me. We could have been very happy together, but I think I'm going nuts. Again. I can't even write this note very well. To think that I was going to get pregnant in this mental state. I don't think I can handle it. Good-bye, Michael, I can't think of anyone who could have made me happier than you. Live a good life, baby. With eternal love, Theresa.* He remembers, of course he could remember. *My life has got all the elements of really bad fiction. Then again, everything did happen to me.* He keeps looking around, but he can't find Xavier's kiosk. Instead, the thought of the stranger from before invades him. In his mind, they do seal the deal in the restroom cubicle, marry on a beach, and adopt three kids from Africa. In his mind, another thought assaults him. The stranger must still be around somewhere. So, he acts upon the need to get out of the market. But in the middle of the street, in a split second, he's flung into the air and cracks his head open after hitting a lamppost. An unseen Honda Civic '96 hits him, and he dies with a smile, thinking of a stranger and a weird connection that could have been. That's all he needed.

And he dies with a smile, thinking of a stranger and a weird connection that could have been. That's all he needed.

Damien reads Antonio's last words as he takes a bowl of soup to his lover, who is clearly famished. It has been too much of a strain for both. It's not easy to live with a writer, much less in the middle of a quarantine, but then, Damien figures, it's far more difficult to be one. He could be angry at Antonio sometimes, but when he sees him in bed, so tired, so vulnerable, what Damien sees is a very small and fragile forest creature in dire need of human help and healing. This isn't the only thing that keeps him besides Antonio's bed, with a bowl of Lipton's soup in his hands.

"Jesus Christ! Honey, why must you always kill your characters? Is there something I should make of that?"

"Oh, baby please, don't be silly. I kill my characters so my readers can best appreciate the life they're given."

Damien is shocked by such a logical, yet cold and frightening answer. Damien knows what his boyfriend means, of course. But he also recognizes some traces underneath, of Antonio's incapacitating fear of death. There's a slight tone in his words, an almost imperceptible quivering in his music box that makes Damien think that Antonio regards life from a higher perspective. Or that maybe he's starting to develop some emotional condition. Either possibility concerns him. Every possibility wins. He can't help but turn his eyes away from his lover to the green wrapped bundle placed besides Virginia Woolf's *Mrs. Dalloway* at the ledge.

I finish my book with that scene, with the writer in bed and his lover nurturing him. I get it published in an anthology on coronavirus stories and, as a way of giving thanks, I send an email to Xavier. Of course, I know I don't have to do that, but for some reason I feel compelled.

> Dear Friend:
>
> It's been a success. I cannot find the words with which to thank you. You've opened

my mind. I'm in your eternal debt.

Yours truly,
Lorenzo

Do not thank me, Xavier thinks as he reads it, *for things do not look so triumphant for you. Live well, friend, for life is such a fleeting thing...*

II

I finish my book with that scene, with the writer in bed and his lover nurturing him. Tormented by the possibility of having invested all this energy and time in writing a story that may fail, Antonio delves into a maelstrom of post-masterpiece-revisionist-paranoia. And if Antonio suffers, Damien almost goes crazy. Still, he stays by his lover's bed, and gently, in those waking hours, forces Antonio to sit back, in front of his laptop, and edit.
"Baby, please, do this. What about everything you've always told me? About polishing your work? This is something you must go through. Now please, pull yourself together and work. This is what you do best.

He kisses Antonio's forehead and leaves the cup of Lipton soup at the table, besides the laptop.

Yes, that's a nice ending. I guess it was a good idea to listen to my editor. I think this revised version is better suited for publishing.

III

Xavier has a busy day that day. Telling fortunes to people who won't listen is a bad thing. Telling them to people who actually want to avoid misfortunes is worse. And he simply cannot care less. Why would people always think he does? He's simply doing his job, a very nice job indeed that granted him tons of stories with infinite possible ends. The perfect complement for a writer.

He lies there, drawing pad and HB pencil on hand, on his black satin sheets spread nicely over the bosom of a very lonely bed. He starts drawing images, first a Honda Civic 96', he's always loved drawing Japanese cars ever since he was a child; then a scene of two lovers sharing a bowl of soup. He then comes up with a beautiful representation of his metal-wired, intricately designed tarot table. There, in the image, is a very lonely young man, raven-black disordered hair, shaved chin, and dark olive eyes. For an instant, he's taken aback by his own portrait. *Am I such a solitary person? No, of course not. They are all with me.* He places the drawing pad and the pencil back on the night table. He grabs the Two of Swords from the deck of cards on his beloved wired table. *Two ways, two endings. Decisions...* He places the cards back inside the green cloth, wraps them in a bundle, and puts the deck on his metal wire table. Then, he takes out his journal and writes in a very beautiful, almost feminine handwriting:

A man's life, and the stories to be told... all gone in the silence of one second, gone like words that come from the sky, and are written on paper... but when all things seem lost in the fleeting turns of too many suns and moons, a new story begins, or perhaps it was not new, but rather existed at the same time, twining together with the first one, or simply existing in its shadow...

The Floating Church

This is the worst drought the island has gone through in about 30 years. Lake Caonillas is already at 37'. If this keeps on, the government will be forced to impose strict measures of water rationing. Leaders of different religious factions on the island had decided to join together in prayer and praises to the Lord, to demand rain. They agreed on next Saturday as the date of what is beginning to be called as "Pray Day."

Climbing up Punta Guilarte is not an easy feat. It has to do with a certain spiritual purification ritual, at a specific time of the year, when the *yagrumos* are reverse-leafed and the avocadoes are too much for just one tree to bear. It has to do with the storm-coming time of the year when people still remember the legend. When the rainy season comes, they say that clouds climb down the stairs of heaven and reach the tip of Punta Guilarte. They say you can jump from there and fly, for the place, in that season, imbues with flight everything that jumps into the abyss.

Doña Andrea prepares to climb the mountain for the last time, putting on a thermal sweater and pants. She looks in her mirror and into her white reflection. She is big, girthy, elegant woman. At mere 5'5" and 193 lbs., she still looks gorgeous, what with her signature pose at photographs: flirty, with her dashing white smile, slanted eyes with mile-long lashes, age lines that greatly emphasize her dazzle, flamingo-red lipstick (either that, or shocking pink), her right arm angled resting her right hand over her right hip, and finishing it with a little fling of hair she doesn't have (she has very short trimmed white hair, which only accentuated her brown eyes and killer smile). She stands in front of the mirror and does the pose. In her mind, she's a *yagrumo* and the storm's about to begin.

"Okay, gorgeous, you are splendid!"

Yagrumos are a mystery, even to the people who inhabit this island. They seem to have a special connection with the weather. People say they can predict storms like any of those so called "weather psychics," who in reality are no more than very old people with arthritis. These trees, however, flawlessly turn their leaves upside down, giving a melancholic effect to the landscape, a tone of spearmint finesse to all that brightness of yellow and limes under a more general green. They turn their faces upon the land, as if too afraid of what's coming. The only thing is, at the time, there's no hurricane in the Doppler's sight.

She looks at the ascending road before her. Doña Andrea holds her chin up, as if not only challenging the majesty of the mountain, but also paying respects to a more powerful opponent that is not necessarily a foe. Punta Guilarte grows before her: a climb of almost an hour and a half. She thinks really hard about what she's about to do. She's going up, but not coming back down. She thinks she's alone at the moment, at the point of starting the big climb, until someone interrupts her carefully thought thoughts.

"Andrea! Hello there, honey, how are you?"

One of her neighbors. One who saw everything that happened, but did not call the police. *How come everyone turns deaf when something like this happens*, Andrea thinks. *I guess it has to happen to you so you can tell.*

"Hey, Andrea! Where are you going at this time of the afternoon? Are you gonna climb up there?"

"Yes, Pinina. I'm going to climb!" she replies and then dazzles the woman with one of her most spontaneous and practiced smiles.

"Honey, when are you coming back?"

"I don't know," she says. Then, Andrea looks back at the woman's face and understands she doesn't mean climbing back down, "Oh, you mean, to my old house? Never. Even less now that I'm filing for divorce."

"Was it that bad? I mean, don't get me wrong honey, I support you and all, but what are you going to do? I mean, he's the man of the house, and... and... and you are not exactly young again..."

"Thanks for that, Pin. You of all people should know how bad it was, you're the closest neighbor I've got. You must have heard everything. In fact, I bet you did. And you didn't call the cops. What do you expect me to do?"

Andrea is at the point of tears by now, but still, she keeps her smile, *yeah, smile! Smile as hard as you can! Until it pains you to smile! Don't lose it! That's your only weapon!*

The other woman lets it go, and Andrea starts the road up to the mountain.

He has been seriously thinking about it. *So, it all comes down to this...* Daniel looks through the window, from his room on the second floor of the house. The lake extends its domains all the way through the mountains, as if were not really a lake but a very wide river. *I'm really gonna miss this*... But he can't stay; it doesn't matter if he wants to stay more than a rainbow wants sun and rain so it can exist brilliantly arching its way from cloud to gold cauldron.

He sits up from his bed and starts packing two suitcases. He puts in the first one 14 pairs of underwear, 14 pairs of socks, 7 jeans, 7 shirts, 7 T-shirts, 7 pairs of shoes, hair gel, toothpaste, toothbrush, a tiny scissor for clipping nose hair, two leather jackets: one brown and the other black, a pocketknife, and a square wooden box with ornate and intricate carvings that suggest some kind of Taino runes.

He then walks down the stairs and goes straight to the kitchen with the second suitcase. In he puts some Campbell's, Chef Boyardee's, coffee, and sugar packages, a can of powdered milk, two knifes, two spoons, two forks, two plates, two bowls, a can opener, pasta packages, export sodas, vanilla wafers, his father's cigarettes, more cookies, a Vitamin C pot, and sunflower seeds. Lots of them. He also puts his whole collection of condoms in there.

Then he goes into his parents' bedroom. There, he opens his father's underwear drawer and pulls out two of Mr. Alejandro's three wallets. He sucks all the money from both, counting a total of $678.00.

"You had this coming, mutherfucker."

He takes one of his baseball bats with him, carrying it with his right hand, the only one free, for he's holding both suitcases with the left one. He opens the front door and looks around. He's really going to miss all this... the purple, hairy *coítre* bushes, the *jacarandas*, the pine trees, the *abetos*, and the giant *caliandras*. All that foliage coming to an end with the one he's going to miss the most: the *yagrumo* tree. Its leaves are reversed. *Storm's a-coming.*

He leaves the front door wide open, throws his stuff inside the jeep, and takes the bat with him to one of his father's cars. He hesitates for a moment. *Is this absolutely necessary?* He waits for a moment until the answer finally comes to him in one of those episodes when you simply cannot fathom what your own life has come to be. *Yes, it fuckin' is.* With that, he breaks out of his limbo and three of the car's windows end up smashed.

"Now we're even."

He steps inside his jeep, turns on the ignition and drives away, trying to begin anew and forget.

The drought is getting worse. We are talking about 30' of water in a lake that used to be able to hold 87'. The situation is aggravated by the fact that a big 67% of the remaining contents on those 30' are mostly sediment.

Andrea feels dizzy. The hot air seems an omen of storms, but there are no clouds. It suffocates her, what with the increasing heights and humidity. All around her are sparse wooden houses and people doing their daily stuff, not paying attention to the woman who keeps climbing, not bothering to see her courage, because it takes courage to run away when you are 56, having been married for the last 35 years and having lost her children to their father, losing also her marriage in the last few nights. She also loses the fear that comes from husbands too drunk to care if they hit their wives. She is sick of that environment, and finally, just three days prior, she files for divorce. It hasn't been easy for her.

"You can't do this to me, Andrea! You can't! I'll get you for this, fucking bitch!" he screams at her as the cops drag him away.

That day she doesn't have anything smart to sass back. She can't even summon one of her devastating, oh-so-practiced smiles. She's lost in her pyrrhic little victory. And Punta Guilarte looms over her like the challenge she needs to get her mind away.

She stops for a moment to catch her breath and contemplate the landscape. Sky's bright blue, imposing its horrible, searing sunlight over the people, slowly turning them into living raisins. The greenery all around her is too dry to communicate anything other than its own thirst. And it's not alone. Andrea is thirsty too. So, she approaches a woman whose radio is on, and asks for some water.

"Good afternoon."

"Good afternoon. Are you doing the climb?"

"Yes," Andrea smiles. It seems this was the only question people from these parts ever ask. "But I had to stop. I'm incredibly thirsty. Can I trouble you with a glass of water?"

"No trouble at all. Hold on. I'll be back with it."

The woman goes inside the cute and cozy-looking green wooden house, leaving Doña Andrea to her thoughts and to what's going on in the radio.

...drought seems to have done it. A church was discovered coming out of Lake Caonillas, due to the recent lack of rain. Puerto Rican historians and scientific experts say that the Church was there before the Americans came in 1898. It seems to have drowned during their

interventions in the making of the lakes that we have now...

"A floating church, can you believe it?" the woman says as she comes back with the glass of water.

"I guess I die happy now that I've seen it all. I bet that church is gorgeous."

"I bet that too. The say they found some Taino stuff under it. Some runes or something. Are you going to 'Pray Day'?"

"I don't think so. No. I'm just climbing for the last time."

Andrea says goodbye to the kind woman and resumes her climb only to see in the distance something strange going on at the top of the mountain. Fog is forming, and clouds, as if it were about to rain.

Daniel has been driving for hours, and he knows he will eventually have to stop. He has been going aimlessly nowhere, just trying to get the image of his father out of his head. He can't believe he has pursued the career his father chose for him, to begin with. He can't believe he has let his father bring that woman to the house, his mother's house no less! He has to go because he's in murdering mode.

"You had it coming!" He can't stop repeat those words.

He's been driving through the highway, speeding a bit more every turn, changing lanes the way you change underwear, speeding more and more until he's pushing at 107mph. It is then that he identifies a very familiar exit some distance away. He slows down and steps on.

Now he has a place to go for a while until he sorts out what to do next. The shore of Lake Caonillas, which he has visited so many times before to clear his mind and purge negative thoughts. By the time he arrives, it's already evening. He turns off the car lights and the ignition and steps out of his jeep. He takes the bat with him just in case he needs it. and the box with the intricate Taino carvings. He can't leave it anywhere without supervision.

He can't see a thing, that's how dark lake areas are in this island. But he's cradled by the silence and the sounds of distant *coquíes* and the constant wind, slightly splashing the lake's water on the shore. He sits on the grass, not quite seeing it but knowing that it's there. He opens the box, and even though he can't see the contents, he knows what they are. He knows the national treasure that they are. He has seen the stones, the ones called "The Taino Alphabet", which have runes carved in them, and which date to the times of the Igneri on the island. The stones have been the contentious punching bag of the Puerto Rican Culture Institute, where they were used as paper and door weights. He knows all this from friends. And he also knows that his father stole them with the help of the bitch of his new wife, even if he lied about.

The fury drains him, and this makes him receptive to the surrounding sounds, which steal him away, and he drifts into sleep in peace.

It's fog. It's a bizarre mist forming out of nothing, for there are still no rain clouds, and the sunlight still pierces. Andrea feels enveloped in a miracle, surrounded by the unbelievable, trying to solve it in her head, but not quite accomplishing it. For she is still thinking of her kids, of the way those fuckers turn against her when their father says, on several occasions, that he's going to kill her. *This is crazy*, she thinks, and that's when she really understands her situation, calmly coming out of her post-divorce shock.

The last steps to the top of Punta Guilarte force her out of her thoughts. She almost slips into the precipice. Suddenly scared, she turns back a few steps and sits down in wait for the fog to disappear. When it does, daylight enables her to appreciate the view. She can see four or five towns from Punta Guilarte. But it's not that. It's the empowering feeling of climbing, and finally escaping the torture of all those years wasted with her asshole ex. On the top of Punta Guilarte, she can finally breathe, even if the altitude makes the air thinner here. And that's when the sky falls down on her. Two icy drops, then five, then a whole deluge bathes her as a gift to wash away her pain; she lets herself be soaked by the heavens of Punta Guilarte, the clouds that come from nowhere, as they always do on this island, letting herself be crushed by the joy of such a beautiful miracle.

The legend comes to her then, the one she's heard when she was but a child, for legends are always heard in those times. After all, they can only be believed by children. When there is fog and rain in Punta Guilarte, the place will let you fly once you jump. It has been engraved in her so deep, as a matter of the purest fact, that she believed it when she was girl. Why not believe it now? She stands tall, and again she thinks this is crazy. But she also knows this is her one chance to see if the legend is real, her one chance to be part of a miracle. So, she jumps. And god, does she fly!

He wakes up because he feels drops of water falling on his face. He rubs his eyes and looks at his watch. It's already 3:09 p.m. He has overslept and feels both dizzy and hungry. But before he can start worrying about either that, or the coming rain, he sees it. Stepping regally out of the water, the most beautiful church he has ever seen. A floating church.

Instantly, he stands up, trying to make something out of it, trying not to think what a miracle is for an old church coming out of the lake because of the recent drought. He rubs his eyes again, completely forgetting his inner circumstance, at least for a moment, and laughs. He laughs hard looking only at the church and to the sky, laughing of joy at the vision that nature has conspired to bring him; he looks back at the church and then back at the sky, laughing harder, until it's so hysterical that he can't laugh any longer, but smiles. He feels the rain coming down on him, and inside him, he thanks whoever's responsible for this. Because rain has waited for him to see the floating church before falling. And before falling he looks back at the sky, and thinks he sees a bird. Until he identifies the figure of a girthy, big, smiling woman. A flying woman. It rains hard then, and he sees nothing else. Not the church, not even his own hand. That's how hard the deluge is. This is how it rains in Puerto Rico. Feeling blessed and still not quite believing his eyes, he steps inside his jeep and drives away, this time knowing where to head with the box full of Taino runes, and what to do.

The Mutherfuckin' Trans Everest

"Dude," Darren tells Varrik off, "you could grow a penis on your forehead, and you'd still not be a man."

"Being a man is more than having a penis," Varrik retorts.

"Says the girl who doesn't have one. Call yourself whatever you want, but don't pretend that we'll all fall for it. Gay men don't like pussy, do you understand?"

"No, I don't understand," Varrik says. "I walk like a man. I dress like a man. I workout like a man. I live as a man. Therefore, I am a man."

"No, you're not."

"I am!"

"No! You! Are! NOT!"

"You reduce sex to a matter of genitals! People don't have sex with genitals! They have sex with the soul."

"Honey, whoever told you that harmed you more than you'll ever know. It's a lie. I am a bottom. How do you think you could ever satisfy me sexually? Think about it. You don't have a penis."

"I have a penis."

"Your clitoris is not a penis, hun. You may call it that, but you are only fooling yourself. Your vagina is just that. A vagina. Also, your strap-on is not a penis."

Varrik is about to explode and hit Darren. No one has ever dared talk to Varrik like that.

"You are the only gay I have ever met who thinks this way. You are getting left behind, boomer."

"Oh, so now I'm a boomer even if I'm not even in my thirties? Great. Listen, you're only fooling yourself. They may not tell it to your face, but no one buys your performance. You are a con woman, and everybody can see it. They don't say it only because they don't want you to kill yourself. Me? I don't give a shit. Gay men don't like bearded lesbians."

"Gay men are transphobic. I get it. Thank you."

"If that is what you decide to take from this exchange, go ahead. You do you."

Darren slams the door. Varrik leaves in tears, with a red face, and fists curled up. They had met on Tinder. Darren's profile sports a "no pronouns people" in caps, yet somehow, Varrik must have missed that. Varrik, Darren thinks after the person behind that profile sends him a private message. He looks at the pic and it's a live rendition of the Legend of Korra's character named Varrik, a dude with a Dalí-like mustache and wavy brown hair. Darren dismisses the message, but the Varrik person insists.

"Ok. Send a dick pic, and we'll talk," Darren types back.

"Sure." The Varrik person sends a dick pic that looks suspiciously like a dildo but engages him in conversation and Darren falls for it and extends an invitation home. And the rest is history.

As soon as Varrik gets back home, he calls the clinic.

"Yes, I'd like to talk to Dr. González-Whippler."

"He's not around at the moment, but may I help you?"

"Yes, I'd like to know the status of Project V-129."

"It's growing healthy. Are you the happy owner?"

"Yes."

"According to the readings, three more weeks and it's yours."

"Is it healthy? Does it look real? Does it look nice?"

"Yes, it does. It's a piece of living art."

"Good. Thank you."

While waiting, Varrik does a lot of stuff to think about something else. Delving head on into work usually does the trick. And working remotely fits the agenda perfectly.

"Tandem Solutions, this is Varrik, how may I help you?"

Two dozen clients per day is a good number for production. Varrik's bosses are happy and must be kept that way. Otherwise, bye bye job, and bye bye testosterone shots.

Mother calls. Varrik answers with a *yes* all her questions: are you taking your supplements? Are you going to all your psych appointments? Are you taking your shots the right day in the right shoulder? Are you taking care of yourself? Are you ok?

"Yes, mom," at the nth.

Varrik looks at the portrait of a man whose look is the target of this process. Some trans people frame pictures of the people they want to look like after the change. An aspirational something to give them goals for the future. To keep them alive. Much in the same way that gay men with AIDS used to be encouraged to set goals for the future. The man in the frame is Tom Selleck, of course. The quintessential referent.

"Do you want to see your new self?" asks the nurse. "The inflammation is over."

"Yes!" answers Varrik.

"Are you excited?"

"Pretty much, yeah. How long have I been here?"

"Surgery was a huge success. It took four teams in four shifts to fix you up. That makes two days," the nurse says while removing bandages from all over Varrik's body. "You've been in recovery for two weeks, though. The surgery was hugely invasive, and you may be still sore in some parts. It's a new body after all. Molded like clay." The nurse smiles. "Shut your eyes for a bit. I'll tell you when to open them."

"Ok." Varrik complies.

"Now."

It's like Varrik awakens to a new self. The jaw has been squared and forcibly seeded with facial hair. There is an Adam's apple, reconstructed from printed cartilage, and it looks good.

"We took all the breast tissue," the nurse continues, "and reconstructed it into muscle because it was healthy tissue, after all, and it would have been a pity to toss it away. That took skill. So, if you like what you see, remember to leave us a good score on Yelp."

The chest looks good too. They were kind enough to seed it with hair too, as well as the armpits, and massive forearms.

"So, we had to take out your womb, ovaries, everything. It's all gone and donated, per your request. You have prosthetic gonads, large size. I'm told you'll get the hang of it, no pun intended, but they may feel weird at first, like something's pulling you down to earth. And the penis…"

Varrik smiles. It's a huge penis, grossly fourteen inches of man meat modeled after some dead Ucranian adult performer who died during Putin's War.

"Do you like it?"

"I do. How does it work?"

"You can pee through it. And when you want to have sex, push this button right here under your right cybertesticle. Here."

The penis inflates and Varrik can feel the pull of blood from the rest of the body. From arms, legs, and head, which go light.

"When you're done, press this button right here, under the left testicle. And there. It'll go down."

The rest is just hair seeding all over legs and butt. Varrik approves.

"How do you feel?"

"I feel like me."

"Good," the nurse smiles. "Let's talk about maintenance. You must have at least four erections daily, to stimulate the tissue. If you don't use it, it will atrophy. As for hormones, you must take a shot to the shoulder every week. It's 2cc of this," she says, handing Varrik a small glass vial of a clear liquid with a pharmaceutical stopper. "Can you handle this part of the process on your own?"

"I think I can, yeah."

The first few weeks, Varrik's penis would not stop oozing pus. The infection spreads to the pelvis and it hurts like hell. Varrik spends several days hospitalized. Once the infection is gone, Varrik is discharged.

Walking like a man while trying to maintain such a huge piece supported by underwear takes Varrik some days to practice. It's like getting to know Varrik for the first time ever. It's like the soul of Varrik was transferred to a new and improved body. Different dysmorphia but still dysmorphia. The hairs on the body create much more static than before. Varrik will have to be careful when opening doors with metallic knobs. Then, there's the Adam's apple. The first week it proves a bit difficult to swallow food or liquid. It's soreness all over the body. But it's a particular kind of soreness, one Varrik had never experienced before: that of phantom aches.

Two months into manhood, Varrik meets a guy on Tinder. His name is Rolo, a biologist for some big pharma. The biggest white boy Varrik has ever seen, built like a white rhino, Rolo works for a viable and functional cure for hiv, hpv, and herpes.

They meet at a streetside bistro named *El Tamarindo*, whose specialty is two-pronged: sautéed pork chops in tamarind sauce and tamarind-over-cheesecake. Rolo eats the pork chops. Varrik sticks to a salad with tamarind vinaigrette.

"So, what do you do?" asks Rolo.

"I am a content creator for a PR company."

Something in Rolo's face changes. Something reveals, for a microsecond, a profound disappointment.

"So, you work for one of those flack companies that manufacture truth for the media?"

"It's more complicated than that, but essentially..."

But he tunes out. Before Varrik can protest, the waiter arrives with their dishes and some champagne.

"For the lovely couple," the waiter says. "Courtesy of the house."

"Oh, dear," Rolo says, impressed.

"Thank you, and please thank the owner for me," Varrik says.

"Will sure do," the waiter replies and leaves with a smile.

They change the topic to movies and the night flows better. Rolo's favorite movie of all times is *The Shape of Water*.

Varrik's is *White Chicks*. They couldn't be worlds farther apart. But still, they go together back to Varrik's, because there is an itch, and what is an itch but a mutual favor waiting to be claimed?

They start kissing at the edge of the gate, then their clothes start flying as soon as the front door, only to kiss hard on the second story, and end up in the bedroom.

"Give me a second, hun," Varrik says, going to the bathroom. Inside, Varrik touches the button under the right testicle, prompting a ridiculous arch protruding from the legs.

"Now, look at you," Rolo says after Varrik comes out. "Looking good."

"Thanks. You're not so bad yourself," Varrik replies.

They kiss again, but Varrik's soreness flares up at Rolo's touch and cries out in pain.

"What's wrong? Are you ok?"

And that is when Rolo really pays attention and sees the minuscule and puny scars under the chest, the ears, and the groin. He starts seeing Varrik like one of those Tousa Tousa male dolls that have detachable penises in different forms. And then, the remaining seems to unravel before his eyes: the squared jaw by adding bone, the fake Adam's apple, the seeded hair that looks too much like a Ken doll's hair... all in all, a bearded lesbian. He pushes Varrik aside.

"Are you a trans man?" Rolo asks.

"Yes, I am a man," Varrik sentences, covering up.

"Right. This doesn't feel right. I'm sorry."

Rolo dresses up and leaves. Varrik is left dumbfounded, with a face that really, really can't understand.

Varrik tries several more times. But the same thing happens with Richie, the skater. And Darío, the barista. And Mick, the mechanic. And Joao, the dominator. Same thing happens over and over.

"Gay men are so fuckin' transphobic. I'm so done with them," Varrik sentences.

"Thank you for coming in su-such short notice, Va-arrik," Dr. González-Whippler ejaculates with a trembling jaw.

"How you are doing, doc?"

"I'm go-good, thank you. And I have ha-happy news! Come with me."

They exit the doctor's office and walk to the left, through a labyrinth of clinical halls and corridors illuminated by that white searing light, and finally enter a glass-walled room, with several plastic cages full of rodents of all sizes. There are mice with ears growing on their backs.

There are guinea pigs with fingers and even hands and feet growing off their spines. And penises that sprout off the bellies of rats.

"There's yours. It's being fe-fed by Trevor."

"Who's Trevor?" Varrik asks.

"The rat."

The poor creature lies on its back all day and all night, as its weight cannot support the human structure latched onto it, sucking its life. There is a rare quality to such a huge flaccid penis, a grey vampiric quality. But Varrik says nothing. This is what it takes. This is the final milestone. The mutherfuckin' trans Everest.

"What will happen to Trevor afterwards?"

"Why? Do you wa-want to adopt a rat?"

"Not really."

"Yeah, that's wh-what I thought."

The Map She Etched in My Head

Lizy's voice feels like a heart attack when she visits me at midnight. The room spins, twists, and twirls, and I'm left gasping for air while she utters every single one of her chosen words: *Cal, I love you.* After that, my sister leaves. I clutch at my heart. It feels like I don't have one anymore, like the beating rhythm of my chest is tied to the sounds my sister makes leaving and I wake up, trembling, my bed wet.

"For fuck's sake, Callum! This is the second time in a week!" my wife whispers irritably after waking up in a pool of my nightmare piss. "Lizy again?"

"Yeah."

"You gotta talk to someone about this, Callum."

"I'm talking to you."

"I mean a professional, Callum."

She always does this whenever she's tired of me. She ends all her sentences in my name, to emphasize how sick she is of telling me off.

"Get off the bed, I'm gonna clean up," I say. "Don't you have fabulous work to do?"

While she showers, I take some Excedrin for the migraine, change the sheets, spray some bleach on the mattress, and let it air. I pick up the phone and make a call.

"Dr. Viera's office. How may I help you?"

"Hi, my name's Callum Rhodes and I'm a patient of Dr. Viera's. I'm calling to check if there's a free space this afternoon."

"Let me check, please. I have an opening at 1:00 p.m."

"Can I get it?"

"Sure thing, Mr. Rhodes. We'll be waiting for you."

Jean gets out of the shower. She looks radiant, her breasts perky and always pointing upward, her pussy shaven, her strange scent between her legs being something like oatmeal, recently caught salmon, cloves, and anise.

"My poor baby," she says, grabbing my cock with her right hand.

"You're gonna be late for your firm. What will your fabulous colleagues think of me, then?"

She withdraws but smiles. She disappears in the walking closet, where she puts on her white silk blouse and her black high-waist tube skirt, along with a pair of black stilettos, no hoses. I get erect just watching her but turn to the mirror when I think she spies me. I look at myself in the mirror. Early forties married to a girl a bit older than half my age, all tatted

213

and bearded up except for my chin, still strong and muscular, still furry like a fox, my hair a long lion's mane. I guess there are worse ways of ageing, but I still apply some Preparation H under my weed eyes.

"Will you be coming home after work?"

"I'll let you know, daddy," she answers with a devilish wink that makes me give her a spank as she leaves. I shower, jack off, put on some jeans, boots, and a white T-shirt and leave for Forge St., a backwoods road way out of the city and suburbs, to open the auto shop. Ty, Miguel, and Yuri must be on their way. We've got eight cars to finish today.

I roll up the garage door, turn on all the lights, the old radio music system in La Suavecita FM 92.1, and make sure the bathroom's clean. Then, some coffee.

"Morning, Cal," says Miguel, a very cool and the youngest of my mechanics. During summer, he hangs out in suspicious jean cutoffs, and he's always talking about the latest pussy he ate. He has a very deep black beard and very dark eyes, and the ladies love him, even though his face and chest are scarred, and he still got some almost visible shrapnel under his skin. You know, like when you're young and dumb, and you stick the tip of a pencil in your skin, and somehow, your body never rejects it, and it stays there, all blue, like a figment of vein that detaches and strays far from its root. I think he was in Desert Storm.

"Whatup, man?"

"It's a meh day."

"Okey dokey."

That's his way of pissing territory. *Don't talk to me today and leave me be.*

Next to arrive is Yuri, the oldest of the pack, and ten years my senior. Over the years living in Denver, he's lost his Russian accent and meanness. He's also stopped drinking recently and now he's always cold. Even in summer.

"Boss."

"I'm not your boss."

He smiles. Behind that Santa beard there's a smile that cares. He's the closest to a dad.

Finally, as always, there's Ty.

"You're late."

"I know. I'll stay late tonight."

"Fair enough. Ok, everyone, I gotta go at noon today, so I'm leaving Ty in charge of closing."

"So, how are you feeling with the new meds?" she asks, her very doctor combination of beige skirt with beige blazer and the most sexless and boner killer wine ruffled blouse. I drown an "urgh."

"I'm mostly ok."

"Mostly?"

"I mean, I'm getting used to being here and being no one."

"You have to be, if you are to stay protected."

"I know," I say. I don't lie. I know the terrible consequences of the program.

"Are you sleeping well?"

"I'm having terrible nightmares."

"How terrible?"

"Bed-wetting terrible."

"Why?"

"It's my sister, Lizy."

"You mean your dead sister..."

"Right."

"And what does she tell you?"

"To find something... I can't make out what she says because I wake up with a terrible ringing in my ear, pissing all over the place, and with a splitting migraine."

"That doesn't sound normal, Cal. How are you feeling *now*?"

"I've been dizzy since I started your meds. That's why I say I'm mostly ok. Like I'm functional, but I also feel all kinda wrong in my body. Like it does whatever it wants. I'm forty, I mean. Wetting the bed at my age? Jesus, even saying it out loud..."

"Cal, look at me. Cal. Cal! There you go. This isn't your fault. You're starting a new decade in your life. No, listen, look at me, Cal, Cal, come on, look at me, it's me. I've been with you since day one, remember?"

I can't stop crying.

"You're entering your fourth decade of life. What happened to you is long gone, so long, in fact, that you don't have to resolve it. It's done. Breathe, Cal. There you go. Mind your breathing. As I was saying, you need to accept some truths and finally deal with them, or you'll get a heart attack."

"They feel more like strokes."

"If they were strokes, you'd be in intensive care right now. You know what? Even a micro stroke leaves a trail. Let me call a friend to schedule a CT scan. Let's see what we find."

She says all this with such a reassuring voice that I forget her horrible taste in clothes. She calls her friend, who happens to work at the hospital nearby, he says that he's got an opening right now, so the good doctor cancels all her appointments and drives me to the hospital herself. The other doctor's a brain specialist. He's also Puerto Rican, I can tell.

"Alright, Cal, I'll be outside while Jaime here does his thing."

She closes the door after herself.

"Ok, man, strip, put this on, and lay on the table right there. Now, I'll be speaking to you on a microphone, but as soon as you're ready, I'll need you to be completely still."

"How still?" I ask because, whenever someone tells me to lie still, my face starts itching like crazy.

"Dead still."

"Can I breathe?"

"Of course. Just not too deeply and not too fast."

I fall asleep.

Jaime wakes me up through the microphone. When he's done, he tells me to put my clothes back on and invites Dr. Viera in.

"Ok... my bedside manner sucks, so here it goes: you most definitely had a stroke. I'm surprised you're not dead. See here?"

My vision kinda blurs, but I make out what looks like strange lights etched in my gray mass. That or voids.

"I'm concerned," he concludes.

"Alright. I'm upping your anti-anxiety medication and giving you something stronger to sleep," Dr. Viera says. "You're too young for this bullshit."

That night, I take the new dose of everything with a glass full of water.

"No-no," says Jean taking the glass off my hand. "Too much liquid before sleep and daddy will wet the bed again."

"That's not funny," I grunt, but she just laughs it off. I top her right then and there and she moans and cries like she's being abused or something, that's her trip, but really, it is she who wears me off like her own personal cumrag. When she's done using me, I doze off and dream again, even though I'm not supposed to, according to the psychotropic manufacturer.

My sister appears before me. This time, she's on her wheelchair, where she spends her final fifteen years, until her eventual death in 2009, when her husband pushes her over a cliff behind our home, wheelchair and all. Her fat body with her fat face caked with pale dead makeup to hide acne scars from teenage years, and her thin hair cropped and combed in a civic lady bun, even though she was barely 35, is found two days later in an advanced state of putrefaction, by a stray pregnant dog, half eaten by rats and birds, and naturally occurring flesh-eating bacteria, I guess. She didn't deserve that. Not because she was wheelchair-ridden, or because she used to be 6'4" before her legs had to be amputated due to diabetes. Her husband disappears soon thereafter.

"Cal."

"What do you want?"

"Cal, find it."

"Find what?"

"Cal!"

"What?" I scream, waking the entire neighborhood up.

"This is becoming a problem," Jean says. "I mean, I get it. I knew you were broken when I met you two years ago. But this is ridiculous. It's affecting me, Callum."

"What do you want me to do?"

"Take the week to deal with this. And the weekend. I'll stay at mom's. You know the number."

"Please, don't tell your mom about this."

"What else will I be able to talk to her about? I'm kidding! I love you, daddy."

"I love you too, Jeannie."

She places a kiss on my forehead and leaves but takes care not to slam the door. This is code for "I'll be waiting for you when you finish sorting this out."

I grab the phone.

"Dr. Viera's Office. How can I help you?"

"Hi. I'm Callum Rhodes. Can I talk to the doctor? She's expecting my call."

"Sure."

"Cal? How are you feeling?"

"Jeannie went to stay at her mother's. It's bad. Really bad."

"Calm down. I'm sure this can still be sorted out."

"Uhm, listen, is there a way for your doctor friend to send me my brain images to my email?"

"I have them. I'll send them to you right away."

"Thanks."

A few minutes later, her email arrives with an attached 477 kB file. I open it. There are four different black and white pictures of my brain, from each side, from up, and from the back. There's a pdf, which I open, but I can't read farther than the word *syncope*. What I can do, however, is place the images together and find a pattern. My sister did this to me. She etched a map of our childhood house in Puerto Rico. The place I leave in 2017 after vowing never to return. The place the program disappears me from.

I take the phone again.

"Uhm, Ty?"

"Yes, Cal?"

"I need you to take over the shop for a few days. Tell Yuri and Miguel."

"Ok."

I step out of the plane. We're still wearing masks even though the plague ended when the vaccine was perfected last December. It's too expensive and people are still freaked.

I pay an Uber to take me straight to the center of the island, to a small mountain town called Morovis, through several unpaved roads, until I arrive at a small box of concrete, the plaster fallen off, the weeds having retaken most of the outside, a locked front door their only obstacle to reclaiming the entire space.

"Is there a way you can wait for me?" I ask the driver.

"Sure," he says.

I have the key to the lock. I've had it since I left this shithole, since my brother-in-law swore to kill me if he ever found me, just before he disappeared.

Inside it's even shittier. Someone must have broken in some time ago. Lizy and Iván's things are all over the floor. The map she etched in my head leads me to my room, under the bed, only it's a box bed because I used to be terrified of whatever could lurk under it, so my sister bought a boxed one in West Indies almond wood, which is super cheap but sturdy. Beneath the mattress, there it is. A single Polaroid of that afternoon.

I am nine. I have a killer fever. My parents brave Hurricane Hugo to buy me some medicine, but they never come back. Weeks later, their car and their bodies will be found in Lake Carraízo, the winds having pulled them over the road and into the deep. My sister Lizy, who had moved in with her husband so that mama could help take care of her, becomes my legal guardian. During the hurricane, she sings the fever away with the only lullaby she knows, a Christian chorus from a nearby Jehovah Witness congregation we used to attend. And when it's obvious that I won't stop crying, she puts her hand underneath my pants and fondles me softly between my legs.

I finally make out her words. *I'm sorry*, she says, over and over until my brains are fried.

"I forgive you!" I shout to the house from behind my mask. I shout to the air, to the very few particles of oxygen left in such a horrible place. I shout at the plague, at the invisible enemies that lurk under our beds and at the back of our brains. "Just leave me the fuck alone!"

Still dizzy, I lock the front door behind me and step out, taking care to look at all sides. You never know when Iván might reappear to try and kill me. I remember this feeling. This is why I left.

I pay the Uber driver again.

"Back to the airport, please. Get me out of here as fast as you can."

The Shelter Thus Becomes the Tomb

It hasn't been long since it started snowing in the Caribbean. It isn't difficult to see white everywhere you look these days. My mom and I moved here seeking some warmth from a quickly approaching ice age. But the Tropic of Cancer is not a tropic anymore. So, Mom, Walter, and I set roots in Luquillo, which is near El Yunque, the kingdom of the ancient Taino deities, and decide that if we're not gonna survive this cold, at least, we'll die close to the gods.

One day, Walter leaves, maybe to answer the call of nature. When he doesn't come back in half an hour, I get worried.

"Mom? Have you seen Walter?"

"Not after he left."

"I'm gonna go look for him."

"Honey, be careful. Blizzard's a-coming."

"I'll be quick, I promise."

I haven't reached the foothill, when I'm already tired. I should have tied tennis rackets to my shoes. When I get closer to the mountain, I hear a feeble whimper, rather than a bark. I see Walter under a tree. When I get closer, I see that he's having trouble breathing.

"My poor baby. I'll take you home right now."

But the wind picks up and makes that horrible sound before it all turns white, and I can't see anything. I carry Walter in my arms and try to get him warm inside my coat, but I'm shaking myself. We need to get beneath the forest canopy.

I spot an amazing tree a few meters north. It's a ceiba tree, one of those ancient beings from the times of the Arawak, with their thorny exposed roots and trunks. The giant opens its roots for us, so I go on my knees and dig the snow out with my hands, while trying to cover my baby.

As I dig, I am able to create a makeshift shelter with walls protected with a curtain of intertwined roots from the times in which this was a rainforest. Outside the blizzard rages on. Mom must be worried sick. I keep Walter as warm as I can, even blowing hot air inside my coat.

"It's ok, Mikey. I'll be fine," he says. His voice has been roughed up by the years.

The last snowflake falls in silence two hours later, the last remnant of a weather violence we humans brought upon ourselves. I grab Walter within my coat and try to exit. But that's when I really look at him. A dog ain't supposed to talk. Walter has been dead for hours. And I don't know if I have the heart to come back home. The shelter, thus, becomes the tomb.

Katayama Fever

He smiles at me with his crooked upper left front tooth. Another shines gold in his mouth. I look at all sides trying to find out if he's smiling at *me*. I am a squalid thing, an insignificant sophomore looking for a place to fit in a very small college. A high school of a college. By the time I look back, he's not looking anymore, so I go inside the biology classroom.

The professor, a woman in her thirties with prominent cheeks that you could pinch if you were a grandmother, and black rimmed glasses, looks down on me for being late. I casually enter as she calls my name.

"Bevins."

"Here, sorry for being late, Prof. Johnson."

"Take your seat. Alright class, so today we'll talk about Schistosomiasis, otherwise known as Bilharzia or Katayama Fever. It is caused by a parasite known as *Schistosoma*. Did you read pages 59-65, which were part of your homework?"

She proceeds to talk about the parasite, now in more local terms.

"The disease is spread by contact with bodies of water that contain the parasites. These parasites are released from freshwater snails which, in turn, have been in contact with animal or human feces. Yes, Halloway?"

"How can you diagnose it in a human being? And is there treatment?"

"Yes, diagnosis depends on egg detection in stool and blood. After detecting possible symptoms, the doctor orders stool studies, which basically means collecting your own shit in super small containers... I'm sorry, I couldn't help it. It's so not funny... right. Now, as for treatment, antimony is used most, and it has proven quite effective. You see, this toxic metalloid, in very low dosages, binds to the sulfur in an enzyme that the parasite needs in order to complete its life cycle, thus killing it. Now, this is what we're going to do today. I want you to actually see the parasite. I've brought some infected water from a river near where I live. I want you to divide in groups of four and see how the parasite looks under the microscope."

The class finishes in tears as poor Marlene Beckham touches the water. Professor Johnson urges her to scrub her right hand with alcohol several times leaving her skin reddened and sore. I laugh, as it all seems surreal. When I leave, he's there. A statue of smiles.

Next day, I find him again, this time at the gym. So, he's a jock. Well then, I can study him in his natural habitat. His lean, muscular body seems to want to hide a couple of prominent hips. Bone hips. Nothing to be done there. He's clad in some black tight jammers that only accentuate his puny ass, bony back, and nice quads. I could lose myself in those quads. He notices me looking and smiles. Again, the crooked tooth and the golden one. I smile right back at him, more out of politeness than anything. He comes closer.

"Hey."

"Hey yourself," I reply.

"What you working on today?"

The absence of the verb "are" irks me.

"I'm doing legs. What *are* you doing?"

"Legs too. Wanna spot each other?"

"Sure."

We move around the place, doing lunges and calf raises, until we finally hit the squat barbell machine. He spots me by placing his body on my back and bracing his arms around me under my pits. I had seen many men spot each other this way. But when I feel his briefless crotch rub against my crack, I sweat so much he asks me if I am ok.

"It's too much weight," I lie.

"Right. It's only 15 pounds on each side."

"Yeah. I'm kind of rusty."

"No problem."

We take turns changing the weights, then finish by doing some abs training. I can see his balls attempting to march out of the left leg of his shorts. Every time I complete a damn sit-up I am rewarded with a glimpse of his hairless balls. At one time he catches me looking at his groin and fixes the leg of his shorts.

"Alright. I'm done here. See you later."

We shake hands, he picks up his gym bag and leaves, presumably to the showers. I follow him from a bit far, through the labyrinthine corridors of the sports complex, behind the Olympic pools. From the water fountain corner, I see him enter through the sauna. I wait five or six minutes and come inside.

The steam drowns me for a minute and my eyes feel as if I were trying to see underwater. I rub my eyes instinctively. As my sight readjusts, I hear the sound of two or three showers. The lockers must be crowded.

"Hey, John. Did you do what you were meant to?"

"You mean, recruit the little guy? Not yet. He'll fall, that one."

"He better. The sacrifice is at 12."

"Right."

Then silence. What sacrifice? What are they talking about? Who are they? I recognize Smiling Guy's voice, but what about the other two? I stay by the lockers, strip, and wrap a towel around my waist. As I cross towards the showers, I notice Forrest and Aimes. So, Smiling Guy's name must be John.

Forrest sports a semi and talks about how he fucked his wife this morning before coming to the gym. Aimes is fully erect and counteracts with a vivid description of his girlfriend's labia. John is flaccid.

"Come on, John, don't you have a girlfriend somewhere?"

"If I did, I'd not talk about her with the likes of you. Not like this."

"Right," Aimes answers. "Asshole."

They finish showering and leave. John stays but turns his back on me. I examine him closer. His hips are definitely feminine, but I can see they are made of pure muscle. It is as if his genes had decided to accumulate pure muscular fiber in that particular section. He could lose all the weight in the world and his hips would stay the same. His ass betrays some hairs in his crack. This one did not shave completely. And I wonder why.

He turns off the faucet and looks my way. He smiles while toweling dry. I smile right back at him. My erection is already purple. I make no effort to conceal it.

"Workout intense, yes?" he asks, again reverting to non-verb usage.

"Yes, it *was*."

"You a bit intense down there too?"

He doesn't wait for my response, but instead moves closer and locks lips with me. I'm taken aghast but I let go. I feel the taste of metal from his golden tooth. He undoes his towel and rubs his erection against mine.

"You so hot."

I place my hands on his solid butt and squeeze. He opens his legs and lets me insert a finger. His anus feels cold. He returns the favor and inserts two digits in my ass. I jump, but he holds me tight, in place, like a statue, a shape of freedom gone into rock, marble, or concrete. I am a statue in his hands. Immobile. Concealed. Malleable only through his will and intent.

"If you want, I could get you into the frat."

"I don't want to be a frat member."

"I wouldn't haze you. I'd take you to the river and make love to you the whole weekend."

"Not interested."

"Come on."

"You may convince me later."

And then, he kisses me harder, tosses me to the floor and penetrates me without foreplay. I kick, punch him on his head and try to scream, but this time I'm a statue of regret, held in by powerful hips whose use I find out in the most terrible way. I start crying, as his penis feels like a knife. A sword that cuts through vegetation in a jungle, my anal lining the savage green. As he rapes me, all I think is that I will bleed out. I bite his fingers, but they feel cold, and he just fucks me harder, cutting me harder, because he knows. He knows we're in that *Seven* scene, in which the killer forces a john to fuck a prostitute with a sharp knife penile prosthesis. I'm the sacrificial whore.

He releases me only after emptying himself twice or thrice. He cries loudly and walks to the shower again. I can't get on my feet. He comes closer, grabs me by the hair and forces me on my feet.

"No word to anyone about this. Understood?"

I don't reply. He slaps me.

"No word to anyone about this. Clear? CLEAR?!"

I nod silently. I feel warm beads trickle down my legs. It feels like blood. Its consistence, the not-so-watery, not-so-iron-like, more or less thick state of it. And the smell. It's unmistakably metallic.

"Squat down and poop."

I obey and bear down. Gushes of blood and cum make their way out of my system.

"Good. You alright now. Drink up."

He pisses on my face.

"Open your mouth. Drink up. Don't make me make you."

He grabs my hair again and I let go. I'll have to change campus, call the police, do something.

"Swallow. It. Down."

But when the golden trickle falls down my throat, all my plans to call the authorities go down the drain with the blood and the cum. I am a statue of fear and resignation. And he is my master.

I don't see him again in three weeks. One Thursday I meet him as I come out of English Lit. He smiles a drunken smile. Drunken master sculptor. The smile reels me in.

He walks to the back rooms that no professor uses. They are too cold and noisy. The old Parisian lady used to teach French there, until she died in class. I'm too enthralled not to follow.

This time all resistance abandons me. He pulls down my pants and briefs and bends me over the credenza. No spit. He enters me like he did in the showers. The very air shall be my lubricant if air can behave so. It can't and again the knives, but I'm his sculpture once more, a statue of nerves. He may yet kill me. Or worse. He may reach for my intestines and pull them out. And kill me.

He erupts inside and decides to take a leak in my guts.

"You so beautiful. And mine. You so mine."

"I am," I reply, without intending to or even understanding why I did.

"You thought about what I said. You going to the river with me this weekend?"

"I am."

"Good."

He lets go and leaves. I stay there. Pants down, piss, cum, and blood leaking out. I'm his whore.

That Friday I wait for him at my dorm. He picks me up in his red Honda 96' and I step in, silently, solemnly, and religiously. A lamb statue to the slaughter of forgotten stones. We drive in silence all the way to the national forest. He says there's a running water pond there but says no more. Every once in a while, his hand finds its way to my legs and inside my shorts. I offer no resistance. He plays a bit with my foreskin. His fingers talk to it. The conversation is one-sided, a telepathic display of dominance. His thumb tells my dick to step up, turn its curve to the left or the right, or even up. I'm a malleable would-be statue of clay.

When we get there, there are several cars in the parking. I panic. He steps off the car, opens my door, and grabs me by the hair. He guides me like this through the rocks. I don't protest. I'm a statue marionette.

We climb in silence, until we reach a stagnant pond people call The Fear. All his frat brothers are there, Aimes, Forrest, Wilkinson, the Debs brothers, Arlington, Barnes, Buchanan, and Johnson. They are naked and erect. John takes off his clothes and rubs his cock until the erection is satisfactory.

"Take your clothes off, or we'll rip them off you," Forrest sentences.

His skin shines with the bit of sun that squeezes from the dark clouds and mountain fog. We are deep in the forest, I realize. I can't escape. They will kill me and not even my stench will reach the authorities. No one will know I died. And I accept it. I am a statue of fate.

I take my clothes off and stand there for judgment. Immobile.

"Step into the water."

The murky pond scares me a little. The water feels more like ooze, and I know this will be it. Schistosomiasis will get me. I'll need a month in the hospital after this.

"Submerge."

I close my eyes and let go. The scene of the hobbits in the Dead Marshes comes to mind. Something will grab my feet and I'll become one more corpse to populate nature. A statue of spirit, of ghost, that will nourish the water and the snails, and the shit of the earth. However, a pair of hands rescue me and drag me to the surface. I vomit.

"You alright. Tough part's over. Now comes delight."

They grab me and take me to a circle of grass. I am prodded, touched, probed, squeezed, and grabbed in ways that make me go red in my ears, but I am gone. I am cold. Even my anus feels cold. And I revel in my lack of shivering. I am a statue made.

They fuck me and piss on me as they fuck me, and piss in me, and trade friendly fire, and piss on each other as they fuck me. We are a moving pond of fear. I and I start feeling feverish as they finish. They throw a bucket of water on me and leave for the night. I'm left there, with John watching over me. I can't move.

"Two more days and you'll be one of us."

I am a statue of silence.

Next day, they submerge me again in The Fear. This time, water from the pond is deliberately poured into my intestine via a makeshift enema. They do intend to kill me.

I am thoroughly raped again the entire day. John sits on my erection for a change and rides it until I cum. Then he commands me to open my mouth and drink his piss along with the rest of his brothers'. I am a grail statue.

On Sunday, they wake me up again with piss. They don't submerge me in The Fear anymore. Instead, a worse nightmare ensues. I am made to lie of my back on the grass. Then, they take turns emptying their vowels on me. The stench of shit is too much, and I pass out. When I come to myself the darkness makes me realize that my eyes have been closed. I am unable to open them. Instead, I keep feeling as they crap on me. Sometimes, it feels like swirls of warm cream are carefully poured on my abdomen, other times hot diarrhea is sprayed all over my face. At all times, soft hands caress me and seem to mold their shit around me. I am a statue of feces, being made into something valuable to them. They laugh and crap as they work like dung beetles. And all I can think of is that I am a statue born again.

At some point I am taken by soft hands and drowned in water. When I open my eyes, I see I am being washed anew. They are all there, in a clean pond: crapping the water that will reach the citizenry but cleaning me.

They take turns kissing, rubbing my purple cock, sucking me off, and riding me as they cum. Then, they drive me to the ER and drop me off like a statue of scum.

I am hospitalized. Katayama fever. The doctor marvels at just how far the infection has spread in only two days. I'm left temporarily blind in the left eye, and one of my kidneys is a bit damaged.

"Just where the fuck did you go swimming?"

I reply something like "the fear" but I can tell she doesn't get it and I don't care enough to explain further. The same way I tell this story, without caring to explain further.

Two weeks later, I am released from the hospital with a nasty warning not to visit any of the rivers on the island ever again. When I get back to the campus, the guys look at me and nod. I am a finished statue of fraternity.

Our Love Is Like Anime

"What I want to do," Reuben says as he turns his bearded visage towards me, "is use your hiv+ cum as ink to draw portraits of religious bigots and homophobic politicians." We're at the bookstore café, one of those up-and-coming literary businesses that blossom in Puerto Rico in the 2010s. The bookstore cannot survive without the café, and the owners hold to the idea of rescuing readers from two or three generations of school deserters.

I look at him perplexed while Steph, the adorable barista, brings us our cups of jasmine tea. She is thin, clad in strange black skinny clothes, half her head shaved, the other wielding a powerful mane of wavy black locks. The tea brings me back to Reuben's idea, which is good. The timing is also great. The energy, however, is off.

"I don't know. I'm not feeling it."

"Well, we've got a couple of months, so why don't you fill this vial, just a bit every day, and we'll talk later, yes?"

"I guess... Listen, Reuben, I am very anal about my work. What I mean is... I'm very strict. I like professionalism above all else. I will work on this, but I expect you not to disappear on me. Do you understand? I've got me no time to waste on shit that won't see the light of day."

He tenses as Steph comes by to withdraw our empty teacups. His super thin frame, like a hairy worm, or hairy spaghetti, scans me with those intensely black eyes. Cosmic, obsidian Guayama-*brujo* eyes. The tendons that hold his neck in place pierce through his latte skin.

"Sure." That's all he says.

Next day, I receive a text message.

"Are you jacking off? Can I tape you while you do that? It'd be nice to record the process…"

"Sure," I type back.

"Excellent!"

That afternoon I receive him at my apartment in a black bathrobe and white briefs. He brings his camera, tripod, and a thousand cables that make me stumble more than once. I hate cables. In my apartment, every single cable is tacked to the iceberg blue-white walls. For the same reasons, every furnishing in the apartment has wheels and space to clean easily underneath. And every piece of furniture, save for the book stands, is small. I need to feel I have space to walk and breathe.

Reuben stops at the jellyfish tank, which contains my young *musume*.

"That's Momongo," I say, while I disrobe.

"He's beautiful."

"*She*. Momongo is the only woman I can stand."

He looks at me with a puzzled expression. Momongo, after all, just swims and floats all day, not having to care at all about performances and relationships. Or sex.

At this point, he's already recording.

"Do you mind if I play something?" I ask.

"Not at all."

I go to the turntable and put Lana del Rey's *Honeymoon*. I sit on the sofa, touch myself through the brief, peel the backside a little, and finger my smooth hole. One finger, three fingers, the whole hand, all the while massaging my member. Blood trickles out of my ass. I catch a glimpse of discomfort in his face. Then his tongue comes out to lick some sweat around his lips. His discomfort excites me. And Reuben's camera gets it all.

"This is awesome," he mutters.

I grab some blood and smear it all over my face. Something about the metallic scent sends me through the roof. My erection jumps to its full potential. He moves fast and places the vial's opening against my urethra, trying to suck in as much as he can, as I don't cum in ropes.

"How was it?" I ask.

"Genius. The video itself is a piece of art. This is gonna be solid."

"Great."

I take a shower while he picks up his stuff.

"Same hour tomorrow?" he asks.

"Sure."

"Then, can I leave my stuff here in your apartment?"

"Put it all in that room over there," I reply. "Then, take your clothes off and shower with me."

He looks puzzled at first, the way every man looks after such a rewarding yet unsolicited invitation.

The day after is Saturday. I have a text from Reuben. He says that he wants to record the entire weekend. I respond in the affirmative and a thumbs up. The day is cloudy, the light soft. There's too much noise around. Ever since the hurricane, Condado feels noisy, heavy, broody, like something bad's a-coming. It's not just the power plants. It's also the chipping hammers. And the tourists. Fucking tourists. It's so noisy that I don't read anymore in this apartment. I have a wall-to-wall, ground-to-ceiling library, with more than 2,500 books that I will never read, because the noise has violated me so much that it has robbed my desire to open a book and read. And my capacity to do so. But I still keep them for a reason that still evades me. Décor, perhaps.

"Can you read something while you jack off?" Reuben asks.

"No," I respond curtly.

"Oh, ok," he says, and I keep jacking off, trying to sell to the camera the idea that I like touching myself in ways other than the ones I have touched myself all my life. Reuben wants to see originality, talent, something, anything that can be edited into art for one of his installations. I go limp at some point because I'm not inspired.

"Are you ok?"

"Nope."

"Wanna talk about it?" he asks without putting down or turning off the camera.

"Nope. I just don't think this part is working out," I finalize. "I think I'm just gonna jack off on my own, fill your vial, and be done with it. Does that work for you?"

"Sure. Whatever makes you comfortable," he answers, but I can tell that he's disappointed. I couldn't care less.

I make to grab the PS4 remote control to either play or watch something.

"You can close the door after you," I say and he finally fucking leaves.

I try to write something that day. I feel like it cannot dusk tonight without an offering of mine to the world, to life, that can justify my existence. But I can't. Have you ever had the desperate drive to feel something, anything, and you just can't? You can't even describe what you need, because first, you would have to know what you have lost and when, and by the time you realize you have lost something all these years, well, it's too fucking late. What did I lose? What did I love?

I do the exercise my therapist gave me for homework during our last appointment. Name three things that you like to eat: burgers, apple pie, and fries. Name three colors that you like: periwinkle blue, emerald green, ochre. Name three countries that you will visit next year (as an aspiration): Finland, Norway, Iceland. Name three things that are true about you: I am a good person who has done terrible things, I am sorry to exist, and I miss my husband.

The exercise is supposed to bring me to here and now, to help me refocus my energy on the present, and to prevent my mind from going haywire with little, imaginary narratives of pain. But it doesn't work because my husband died recently, after 15 years together. It doesn't help that we were happy. It doesn't help that I know that I did everything in my power to make him happy and give him a good life. It doesn't help I had the chance to say goodbye, and even sing him his favorite song, Pandora's rendition of Juan Gabriel's "*Adiós, amor, adiós, mi amor, te vas,*" while he passed to the next plane. *Goodbye, my love, goodbye, my love, goodbye.* None of it helps because he's not here anymore. It's been only a few weeks, and already you cannot remember his voice. And you panic. *Goodbye, my love, goodbye, my love, goodbye.* His face is still fresh in my mind, but his voice is gone. And so, it's not true that he is still with me, in my memories. *Goodbye, my love, goodbye, my love, goodbye.* If my memories of him are what keeps him alive, his flame somehow still alight and burning, then the flame is about to flicker and die in the cold.

So, instead of writing, I try to make urban sketches. I have taken many pictures of San Juan and have sold a few of my watercolor sketches. Today, I try to embody the image of the Music Conservatory in Santurce, but I can't. I don't have the energy. Maybe the piano? Maybe I can play my favorite tunes, and everything will, at least, start to be ok? But, nah. Not even that. There's a hole in my heart and it feels as if the tissue were being disintegrated hour by hour an inch;

me heart feels as if the lining will give out in a few hours, and my beats push the contours of the muscle like bubblegum to its farthest. A heart attack is on its way soon.

I try getting a job. At the age of 44, getting a second job should not be an impossible feat. After all, I'm really good at my first job, and thus, my employability is high. I find something in a translation studio led by millennials. I resign after only two weeks. Nothing satisfies this yearning. Nothing helps me breathe better. Nothing appeases the cannon hole in my chest. And the pain hurts worse.

Momongo is a present. She wasn't supposed to survive from the moment my husband Robbie catches her in a beach in Cairns, during our last trip to Australia. Irukandji jellyfish are extremely small and fragile and can get hurt and die by even touching the walls of a fish tank. Robbie builds a special tank for her before he even attempts to catch one of its ilk. The tank must have a soft rotational, centrifugal force, so that a soft current is always carrying the jellyfish around, without it ever touching the walls. So, the tank has to be circular, in the form of a donut. We pay top dollar to bring it to Puerto Rico via a special ship. In the end, Momongo is home with us, hanging from one of the walls.

Robbie, however, develops Irukandji syndrome pretty soon after we land on the Island. It is weird because he is never stung during our trip, and the doctors can't find nematocysts or stingers anywhere on his skin. Yet, his body hurts everywhere, in unison. A symphony of ache. Since those symptoms were supposed to appear barely two hours after exposure, he is hospitalized. When it is obvious that we won't get better, he asks for my presence.

"Here, papi. These are all the usernames and passwords for all the utility bills and bank accounts. It's all here."

"You're saying goodbye," I am able to reply.

"I am saying goodbye, yes. Flame's about to go out."

"I love you more than life, more than me."

"I love you too, babe."

And he expires with Pandora's song in the background, that is really a cover of one of Juan Gabriel's.

"Here," I tell Reuben from the gate as I pass him a glass vial with all the cum I've accumulated from the last month. I don't even open the gate for him.

"You know what?" he asks from behind the gate. "I was thinking that maybe it would be awesome to find someone with a glass eye and have him fill the glass eye with your cum and put it on as part of a performance."

"Ok. First, ew. Second, glass eyes don't work like that. Third, possibility of infection much? Nah. Stick to your original proposal, please."

He is shaken by my words.

"I want to see portraits of the governor," I push deliberately, "Wanda Rolón, geez, there are so many bigots, where to start?"

But he is still shaken and that pisses me off. His face is the one of a person who had a powerful idea for a minute, yet quickly becomes dust because it can't be executed. His is the face of being forced to leave a good idea in the realm of ideas. He freezes. This is why I fuckin' hate millennials.

"Ok, I did what you asked me to," I interrupt his frozen state. "I helped you. Goodbye, now," and I shut the gate after me.

One day I wake up with a certain fear among a sea of phobias. If I don't get out of my shell and start making friends soon, I will find myself alone in this world. Maybe that's the pain in my chest. A yearning for something as simple as connection, just to stay alive. Just to exist. So, I invite some of my remaining friends over:

    The dark guy with the crystal eye, whose eye everyone thinks will fall off with each pounding of his ass. This one I'll call Poet.

    The long and curly haired friend who performed with honey and feathers at a Christian assembly against marriage equality, whom I'll call the Dancer.

    The Cuban Dwarf with a pompadour who grew up with nothing and ended up stealing money from the Government of Puerto Rico and his group of "kikis" or *it* friends.

    The friend who was a waiter, but suffered an injury during Hurricane María, was not able to ever work again, and in a couple of months, aged to look like a 50-year-old 30-something gay. This one I'll call the Schlemazel.

    The two gym daddy tops who are sick of being together but can't man up and tell each other. These two I'll call X/Y.

    The insidious gossip queen who knows everyone's business and tells it all in his stand-up comedy show at the old coot gay bar *Zal Zi Puedes*. This one shall be called the Professor.

The friend who got told off for almost having sex with a kid that he mistook for an adult, as he's legally blind in his right eye. This one is the Creep.

I open the doors to my apartment to all these guys, and we all dine, and talk about life after the pandemic, and how it all changed, and how it mutated us. Yes, we talk about our mutations. And after crying, we all kiss, and touch, and probe each other. Poet fucks X/Y duo, who are no longer exclusive tops, while the Professor takes a pissing from the Creep, while Schlemazel fucks Cuban Dwarf while fingering the Dancer.

For a minute or two, I'm in heaven. With every caress from every friend, it seems that the hole in my chest can finally start to fill. But it's only an instant in a blasting river of time. And the window's gone. And sure, I cum and we all cum, and we are all the better for it, and our friendship is strengthened, and the spiritual fiber than makes our cells tangible and which forms our very existence, this quintessence is also tempered and empowered. But... the hole is not filled, and the aches resume.

"Everyone, out," I cry softly, but firm enough for everyone to take notice and leave.

I look at Momongo's huge donut centrifugal tank. I take it all in with my eyes, the hundreds of books in the wall-to-wall book stands, the bright walls, the minimalistic furniture, Momongo herself, tiny, puny Momongo. I punch the tank once, twice, thrice until the cracks cede, and suddenly, a tidal wave engulfs me in my apartment, and I feel a sting.

Peter Frampton's Guitar Gently Weeps

It's still dark when Luis parks his blue car at the sidewalk of a historical building in The Islet, a strip of land connected to the rest of the island by a tiny bridge. He opens the office and starts work at 6:00 a.m. By the time Alistair arrives at their translation studio, it's already seven something.

"Morning, Alistair. How you doin'?"
"I'm meh."
"But you just got here from vacations."
"Yes, I know. I don't like taking vacations because I always return disoriented. How are you, man?"
"I'm ok. I finally finished the divorce stuff..."
"I'm really sorry about all that. Jackie seemed like a great woman."
"She is. We're not divorcing because we don't like each other anymore. It's a bit more fucked up than that."
"Right." That's Alistair's platitude.
"Right," Luis repeats. "So, this is what you've got today. Judge Torres González called yesterday requesting translation of an article. I already assigned it to you, so check your email. And don't feel disoriented. I took over your work while

you were away, finished, and sent it. You're welcome."

Alistair makes this weird smile he makes like *man, you freakin' rule and I love working here* and Luis just laughs because, more than anything in this world, he loves feeling like an eternal employee of the month. The former sits on his side of the cubicle and sleeve polishes the picture frame of him, his wife Rebeca, and their two kids. He does that whenever Luis's divorce comes out as a topic of conversation at the office. He turns on his laptop and starts working on the article by the esteemed judge which will be featured in the island's premier legal quarterly. They type the rainy and windy morning away mostly in peace, a peace that Luis cannot feel now even in the solitude of his apartment, and a peace Alistair can never have as soon as he gets home and his two little howlers come screaming to hug him. They consult each other every once in a while, but they mostly do their job in silence, until Luis plays a song on his computer.

"Ah, Peter Frampton," Alistair interjects. "That's a fuckin song, man. Great choice!"

"I like his cover better than the Beatles original. Glad you like it, buddy."

Alistair inhales proper. It's his way of resetting his brains to refocus on the text. He catches a whiff that grabs his attention. *Is that Ck?* Alistair thinks. *But... I thought you had stopped wearing it because your wife hated it. Oh. Now I get it...*

At 2:05 p.m. the rain stops suddenly, wanting to award them a five-minute respite. At 2:10 p.m., the ceiling of the office falls in pieces, they fall from their rolling chairs, the computers fall too, and they're shaken violently from side to side along with the entire island, by a 9.8 earthquake.

They wake up to debris and part of the ceiling down, but at least they're okay and the building's structure has held true. Luis immediately makes for his cell phone, while Alistair desperately looks for his among the rubble.

"I've no signal," Luis says.

"Me neither. You okay, man?"

"I'm good. You?"

"Yup. I'm gonna step outside, see if I can get signal."

Outside, it looks like they were teleported to another reality within the multiverse, in which the island was broken in half by a nasty quake. Except it soon dawns upon Luis that this is his universe and his reality. The street and sidewalk show missing chunks, as if an invisible giant had eaten the city with his cruel teeth and left it for carrion birds to finish off. *Please, let the bridge be there.* Most buildings are down. And his ears are drowned in the screams of the living looking for children, crying for their spouses, as the collective heart of this city shouts the loss of more than five thousand people on The Islet alone. His Asperger's and the excess of stimuli pushes Luis back inside.

"How does it look?"

"Like the end of the world."

"I can't get Rebeca or the kids."

Luis suppresses a scoff and turns his face to the floor, so that Alistair can't read him. *Please, let the bridge be there.* His entire body language screams "they're dead, man!" but he doesn't say it.

"Listen, I'm gonna go somewhere high and see if I can call my family. Wanna come with?"

"Sure. I think Torre de la Reina is still standing."

But most of the buildings are down. *Please, let the bridge be there.* They walk briskly on what used to be sidewalk, which is now a serpentine gravel path. Everywhere they go they hear people crying, and shouting, and calling, and asking why. Alistair and Luis finally get to the entrance of the only building left standing. They pass the surfers' shop, its windows shattered. Two men are taking money from the register, beach clothing, and surf boards. Others smash the windows of the cars parked on the street, in search for money, radios, car batteries, food...

Alistair and Luis climb the stairs like so many others. Everyone wants to see if the earth still stands. Luis and Alastair just want to see the bridge.

On the rooftop, Luis gazes silently upon the destruction. Alistair whimpers and falls on his knees. The only bridge to the rest of the island lies under the sea, and not much can be seen of the rest of San Juan. Most of the buildings lay in waste. It's all flat. He hits his cellphone with the tips of his fingers, as if he could force it to work.

Suddenly, people point to the north shore, as the waters retreat from the canal between The Islet and the rest. Some scream. Alistair cannot stop hitting the cellphone and cursing in frustration, so Luis yanks it away, and searches for Rebeca's number.

"You're a cool character, aren't you?" Alistair says with frustration as he tears his cellphone back.

"I'm sorry. Just trying to help."

Alistair says nothing. His face goes paler than cotton, and he's not even white. The line sounds busy and the call drops.

"We have to stay here until the aftershocks are over."

"What aftershocks? What are you talking about?"

Luis points to the Atlantic Ocean, to their north, as a giant wave looms in the background.

"We're high enough, Luis," Alistair responds dismissively.

The way the tsunami eats another chunk of island, however, puts the fear of God in him. The entire waterfront is gone in seconds, and so is a great portion of the park. The hotels had long been swallowed by the ocean. This is what happens when you build your house on sand. They turn to the rest of the city beyond the new canal and observe in silence as the wave deletes even more land. Their eyes are watching God.

"What are we gonna do, man?" Luis asks, when, suddenly, a couple of people jump from the rooftop to their deaths. "Da fuck are y'all doing?" Luis cries, as if he could pull them back from or stop them from running off into the void.

Alistair just pulls him into an embrace, and they cry themselves to sleep.

The sun burns their eyelids. Luis wakes up to find his nose deep in Alistair's beard. The mix of lavender oil and sweat gives him a sense of ease.

"Wake up, man," he says. "Worst's over. We gotta head back."

They solemnly climb down, pancakes in their armpits due to the godforsaken humidity, and exit the building. Tens of suicides lay sprawled on the gravel. Like others, they flee in despair from such sight.

They find the office as they left it the day before. The tsunami did not reach it. Alistair looks for an old radio and batteries. He turns on the AM section. Nothing. In the FM bandwidth, he finds Ultimate Rock 103.3, which stopped broadcasting heavy metal to serve as a makeshift beacon. Radio host Lolo González states the very hard-to-swallow facts: in a matter of seconds, most of the center of the island dropped to the ocean floor, and what is left of Puerto Rico is five disconnected pieces. An island became an archipelago in minutes. *All those people dead.*

Luis and Alistair look at each other with an adjective-less face, the same that humans make after a catastrophe. A face that decides, from the magnitude of the disaster and from earlier experiences, that they're trapped.

Luis struggles not to cry. Alistair sobs in a corner. It's strange to watch such a tall and lanky man in his early forties cry with such despair, so Luis tries not to.

"We can't stay here for long, you know that, man?"

"I know."

"We leave tomorrow, if you're ready. I'm not leaving you alone."

"Thanks," is all Alistair can say before falling into a deep sleep.

Luis steps out. It's dusk, and nobody's on the streets. He walks across and climbs down the cliff that used to be there, which has been reformed and softened by the tsunami, leaving a shallow beach. He takes his clothes off and washes in the water. Others are doing the same. Some put their clothes back on before they leave. Others don't. He does. *There's no reason to hasten the loss of humanity by abanding modesty.*

He wakes up on the floor, next to the couch, from which Alistair looks at him with piqued interest.

"What time is it, man?"

"Almost eight. Hungry? Here."

He gives Luis a bag of Doritos and a bottle of water from the office kitchen.

"We've to find food," Luis probes.

"Yup, we'll have to take care of each other from now on," Alistair sentences with the deepest sadness.

Despite himself, Luis smiles. Alistair smiles too.

"You and I against the world?" Alistair asks.

"You and I against the world, man," Luis retorts.

They make two backpacks with what little food and water they've left, toilet paper, napkins, and some clothing they had left in the office for times like this. Then, they close it with chains and padlock, and walk northwest. The air is enveloped in the scent of death, like putrid guava in the humid tropical sun, and the caws of black grackles. Good thing they took masks. They cover their noses and mouths and climb the historic streets to find people killing each other with fists, machetes, and guns.

"We need to head back."

"Head back where, Luis? This is all there is."

They stay under cover of rubble for two hours, while the herd of more than 100 people decreases by rite of duel and blood, to a single guy, who, having one bullet left, takes the gun to his right temple and pulls. Alistair and Luis watch with frowns of pity, disgust, and pure unbridled sadness. This is what is left for them to live. This right here.

Before dusk, they find a building left standing because it only has two stories. No one can be heard around, even though the scent of putrid guava permeates, something else Luis and Alistair will have to get used to. The gate's open, and they climb the flight of stairs to find several apartments open and empty. They find one that is fully furnished, with a full pantry. Inside the only room, they only find male clothing, size medium, perfect for a tall, lanky guy like Alistair, and a shorter slim like Luis. They wash with some fresh water that the tenant had collected in big plastic containers, presumably for the hurricane season.

"This is perfect. We could stay here," Luis pronounces.

"Yup, we could stay here alright," Alistair says while he unashamedly removes his clothes in front of Luis.

"What are you doing?" the latter asks.

"Might as well since we're bound together now. Take your clothes off."

Luis hesitates but obeys. Alistair is two or three years his senior and seniority still holds some power after the end of the world.

"Here. I'll hold this over you while you shower," Alistair says. Meanwhile, he takes a whiff at Luis's neck.

"I don't think I can give you what you need, Alistair. I'm not Rebeca."

They spend the next weeks like this, holed up like squatters in someone else's apartment, wondering how the survivors are doing. Then, one afternoon, the stench of putrid guava finally lifts. They look at each other as if for the very first time, and before they can put what they feel in words, Alistair and Luis remove all their clothes and just stand there, in front of each other, separate merely by an arm's length, shameless, and defeated, their furry bodies in the full heat of a humid summer and full of brimming desire. Their eyes embrace in what feels like the true definition of connection, the desired destination of a soul that falls from a rooftop only to transcend. From that proximity, Alistair feels Luis's body odor, untouched by the debris and pulsing its true self; the scent of the city kissed by the ocean's sigh, *why does he smell like Rebeca*, a voice calls from beyond to understand that we're just part of a whole that includes us all outside of words. His blood pressure answers. He puts his hands around Luis, the only thing in the universe he can hold on to, the definition of beauty and silence and everything that is meant to be chased in 100 lifetimes. That desire is everything and Luis responds to that. No longer themselves, they become that desire. They kiss, and what starts like a timid stream of heartbeats and rocking movements soon becomes a mayhem of atoms crashing into each other, as if the circumstances that stripped them of their humanity had transformed them into magnets, who can't do more than rub each other's molecules. The battery radio, which Alistair has kept, plays Peter Frampton's cover of "While My Guitar Gently Weeps," and when he starts singing, it's Alistair who pulls Luis' mouth close to his, but then, as Frampton's voice engulfs the air with the chorus, something wakens inside Luis. *Shit, this is gonna happen*, he thinks, while he makes a grab for Alistair furry cheeks and pries them apart. Alistair is shocked, at first. *Ok, this is gonna happen, he thinks. Oh, shit, this is happening.* Then, Alistair touches Luis like he's always known how his body works. After they come, they hold each other for a while, to let their thought patterns go back from shock, to shame, regret, and finally, peace and acceptance.

"I can't believe we did that," Luis says.

"I could get used to this," Alistair says before he seals Luis's lips with his own.

Thunderclap

"Are you telling me that you want to be gangbanged by a bunch of strangers?"

"Yes. Does that bother you?"

"I told you already. No. Let's go then. Tonight."

"Do you think it'll be safe? I mean—to drive all the way to the warm springs at night?"

"We won't know if we don't do it."

They drive in silence the entire hour-and-a-half road to Coamo. The breeze that comes in from the friction of the car's velocity plugs their ears. Marcos thinks that perhaps the silence of words is the result of having gone too far with his petition.

One thing is Charlie's outrageous sexual history; another entirely to imitate some of his boyfriend's greatest deeds. He tries to touch Charlie's hand while the other drives, but there is an absence of sound, and he knows that sometimes a wall can come from it. He pulls his hand back and into the pocket of his gray hoodie.

As they climb down the freeway away from the mistclad mountains of Cayey, Marcos thinks about the time when his boyfriend told him he had been fucked in the warm springs by nineteen guys, one after the other. He thinks about the things that have been left unsaid, the probable facials, the piss circle, the incredible sexual stamina of his boyfriend's sphincter.

And then he turns on his iPod. "Thunderclap," by Eskimo Joe.

"Nah—too depressing, papa," Charlie says, turning it off.

So, it's silence again.

Great.

They pass the Salinas toll station and Marcos shifts in his seat. His ass-ring twitches in anticipation. He imagines walking to the huge lone Ficus tree close to the latrines, finding a horde of males in heat—as in his boyfriend's tall tales—and satisfying them with his cute, little hole. He twists uneasily at the pain that he will feel.

"The more pain you feel, the greater pleasure it will turn into," his boyfriend had once told him. He imagines the feeling of being hosed up with sperm and his groin protests against his stonewashed jeans. He really wants it. His chest grows heavy with the rush of blood as they turn at the school to the left. The wait gives him pain. In a way, he wants it to be over already. The way his knees jump give him away.

Charlie warns, "You know, you should take it easy, papa. This here is a lottery. There may very well be nobody in there."

"Okay."

"Okay? So, everything is just okay?"

"What do you mean?" Marcos asks.

"Whatever..."

Marcos knows very well. Charlie's probably under the impression that he wants to follow in his steps. HIV had not been enough to scare him away when they had met in the stalls at the park. He had gone right down on his knees and sucked hard on Charlie's 9" x 6" until he put a condom on, took him by the arm to the handicap stall, and fucked him hard.

That kind of liberalism isn't an issue with him either, but Charlie wants it to be that way. It's one thing to be a whore and another to turn a young boy into one. Charlie frowns hard at this, as he continues to drive in silence.

When they arrive, there are plenty of the daylight's residues permeating the clouds. The moon is hidden, but it will not be excessively dark.

"All right, here we are," Charlie announces with a groan.

"Okay," Marcos replies.

"So, this is what we're going to do. There are many cars here. Some of these people may be straight and we don't want any trouble with them. They usually keep to themselves in the pools. But then again, there is action in the pools too, so you may want to trot back and forth between the pools and the Ficus tree. Do you follow?"

"Okay, yes."

Charlie tries not to look frustrated. "Well, you go do your thing and I'll go do mine. And papa, please, be careful."

"Okay," Marcos answers, silently cursing himself for being so nervous as to be unable to say anything else.

"Are you nervous?"

"Very."

"Don't be. I'm going to be around to protect you."

"Thanks, papa. I love you. Tons."

"Me too."

They get out of the car. Charlie opens the trunk, takes off his shorts, and stays in his underwear. He beckons Marcos to do the same. They take off their shirts and grab a pair of black towels. Charlie changes into flip-flops and Marcos follows suit.

As they venture down the half-night road, completely lacking safe illumination, Marcos grows restless. He grabs his lover's hand. The gesture is well received, as Charlie closes his much bigger hand around his puny one. There's lightning far above the town's center, but Marcos cannot hear thunder louder than his heart.

"Damn, I really hope it doesn't rain."

"It seldom does in this town."

As they approach the latrines, Charlie registers movement in the shadows. His experience tells him that, in such darkness, it's always best to look at things from the corners of his eyes. Marcos's experience tells him to leave, that no good thing can happen in such a dark place.

"Let's go to the pools first," Charlie says quietly.

When they climb the ramp, they hear male giggles and grunts. A cloud of moaning, laughter, and virgin's gasps of pain and shock mixed with water vapor from the springs. When they turn at the corner end of the ramp, they see several men in the middle pool going at it relentlessly, splashing water everywhere. Two bears are sitting on top of the hill, observing with lit cigarettes and baseball caps, if nothing else on.

"Ha. They didn't bring their leather. I guess chaps and warm water don't mix," Charlie says with a grin. "Okay pa, you go into the pool and have some fun. I'll go with the bears."

Marcos watches as Charlie leaves with the hairy men; they head into the bushes, further up the hill. Suddenly alone, he jumps into the middle pool. The sixteen or so men who are there quickly turn to look at the innocent virgin who has stepped into their dark realm.

"Sup, *papi*?" asks a black man sitting at the edge of the pool with his hand on his hard-on.

"Nothing much."

"Want to taste this? Come here."

Another thunderclap erupts with light in the distance, not far from the springs. Better decide already, *papi*. It sure looks like the storm's coming this way.

Marcos gets closer and kisses the man's curved ten inches. The latter shoves Marcos's head down, gripping his hair tightly. Marcos protests gutturally but can do nothing to disengage. The black guy forces him up and down until he erupts in Marcos's mouth.

"Swallow it, you lil' bitch."

Marcos obliges, while tears flow. When he's able to pull off, almost sick, he goes to the edge of the pool and throws up. His mouth feels slimy in certain parts, metallic in others. He coughs deeply.

The black man laughs and calls some of his friends in the other pools. He grabs Marcos from behind and covers his mouth while the others play with him. A white man with a mustache plays with his nipples, gently at first, then out for blood. Two guys play at sticking their fingers in Marcos's ass.

They twitch here and there, making sure that Marcos can feel the difference between fingers by their movements. Another guy kisses him hard, brushing each tooth with his tongue. The other four watch as the black man keeps forcing Marcos's mouth onto another man's dick.

Part of him wants to cry out to his boyfriend, another wants to let them rip his ring, to give in to the submission, notwithstanding the hemorrhoids that will surely follow the next day, or the precious blood that's already leaking into the pool. But he can do nothing, even if he were able to choose. They pin him to a corner and penetrate him, one by one, sometimes doubling into him. He's gagged the whole time, either by a *bicho* or a sadistic hand.

Tears continue to roll.

The pain never ends, and pleasure never comes.

"What the fuck are you doing? Leave him alone, immediately!" Charlie rushes at them brandishing a knife over his head.

"Sorry, man. We thought this was what he wanted," the black man replies, abandoning his South Bronx accent for a more Southampton flavor.

"Let him go. Now!"

The men disperse and Marcos gets out of the pool. He vomits once more and cries.

"What's wrong, papa? Tell me, what's wrong?" Charlie asks him.

"They raped me!"

"Hey, we didn't do that shit! He wanted it," says one of the men.

"Let me get you out of here, papa. Let's go," Charlie assures him.

He takes Marcos's arm and places it around his shoulder. Another thunderclap makes itself heard clearly, this time over their heads. Within seconds, it starts to rain full fledge. Charlie carries him all the way back to the car. In the distance, they can hear the other men approach, although consciously trying to keep their space.

They drive away under the deluge, stop at McDonald's for coffee and burgers, and at the gas station in Santa Isabel for two packs of cigarettes and a lighter. They smoke in silence, as rain and thunder follow them all the way back to San Juan.

"Papa, I'm so sorry," Charlie says.

Marcos says nothing. He lowers his seat back, pulls down his wet briefs, inserts two fingers in his anus, and begins masturbating.

"What the fuck are you doing?"

He pays no attention to Charlie and keeps jerking off; he recreates every detail of the scene he has just survived with his own four fingers and comes hard.

"They didn't rape you, did they? Answer me, damn it!" Charlie protests.

Marcos doesn't reply.

He turns on his iPod.

Same song.

Then he cries. Much more.

Even Without a North

So, what if there are only pieces to a story that changes a boy's game? What if the pieces can only be reconfigured through an emotional frame of mind and not through sense or reason? Does that mean that the story did not happen? I often ask myself this.

It's September 18, 1989. I sit on my father's lap while he exchanges blows with my mother, who started the fight.

"You always do this!" she screams at him.

"Do what? Prepare for what's coming?" he asks while protecting me from her blows.

"It's just a stupid storm! Pussy faggot! You know this is important for me!"

"Darla, a fuckin' hurricane is coming! Are you dumb? We can't go to your high school reunion. It's not worth it."

"It may not be worth it for you, but it is for me, asshole!" she screams and lands a nasty slash on his left cheek. Then, while dad cries a bit, still holding me, still protecting me, she gives a final scream, "Don't expect me to come back," and bolts. Her final slam of the door stays with me forever.

"Don't worry, baby," dad says as I start crying. I cry because he is crying. "We'll be fine."

After Mom leaves for her high school reunion, we notice that she has loaded the car with all her stuff. It dawns on me that she really isn't coming back, but I bet my dad knew this a long time ago.

"We need to buy stuff for the hurricane. Wanna come with?"

"Sure," I reply, mostly because the apartment has grown too dark too fast, and I can't deal. It isn't for me to deal with stuff like that at the tender age of nine.

We drive twenty minutes to the nearest supermarket, and already the shelves are emptying at a nasty speed before our very eyes.

"Run," he says, and by that, he means "run and grab whatevs."

So, we run, and while he grabs rice, rubbing alcohol, and cotton swabs, I grab wieners, bread, peanut butter, and jelly. Some fruit left over by the crowd too. This is how I don't think of mom.

We pay and put what little supplies we are able to get in plastic bags. Dad opens the pick-up truck's passenger door and I step in with the groceries.

"Dad, so we really have to go back home?"

"Maybe, we go back, put the groceries where they go, and take a walk somewhere?"

"That would be nice."

But when we get home, Dad gets a call.

"Yeah. She's gone. No, he's with me. No, I don't think she's coming back, no. Do you need any help?"

And then, he hangs up.

"I gotta help Mrs. González tidy up before the hurricane. I'll take a rein check for next storm. We can go to the harbor and watch the waves or something. I promise. For now, be good."

"Ok, dad."

I remember him closing the door and darkness sweeping in again, even with the lights on. I pull on a sweater and sneakers and walk to the beach. From outside, all houses and buildings have their windows covered up with iron or wooden planks. Trapping the dark in. Were it not for the storm, I'd be opening up the entire apartment.

I walk along the sealine, making sure to step on the sand the right way, so that it doesn't go inside my sneakers. There's a technique to it and it was one of the first things dad taught me. You walk like waves themselves, feet in a V shape rather than pointing forward. The darkness creeps in the ocean and the wind picks up, but the hurricane is still not here. This is the sweetest prelude. Some tourists start picking up their stuff to leave. And after a while, I am left alone with a man not that far away. We're the only two on the cloud-ridden beach.

He walks my way, but I don't pay any attention. Dad has asked me never to talk to strangers, so I don't respond when he asks me if I'm all alone here, if my parents are around, and why am I here when there's a hurricane coming. I remain silent, even when he leaves, and suddenly turns, starts running to me, and grabs me in his arms, a black cloth in his right hand which smells funny. And this is where I black out.

The next is a series of vignettes, because, I believe I make intermittent attempts at waking and even getting up, but I am always shoved back, my legs raised in the air, my skin naked to the touch, fading in and out, in and out, in and out, until reason leaves me entirely.

I wake up in a stranger's house. It is almost empty, save for a bed, a chair, and a TV. I am tied to the bed, and I start screaming, but this is when I notice that I am also gagged. The man from the beach appears. He's naked and the smelly black cloth is in his hand. He puts it against my nose, and I fall again into the intermittent rabbit hole of waking and fainting. Again, the vignettes, the comings and goings, the pain in my butt, the blood on my buttocks, the migraine, the disgusting sweat. I don't know how long I am tied to the bed or how long he does to me whatever he is doing to me, but I hear the wind and somehow, I kinda know the hurricane has started.

By the time he's finished, I wake up. I guess I'm getting immune to the smelly substance of the black cloth. And quickly. It stops working on me, and he knows it, but he's done, and I'm still weak, so it doesn't matter if I'm awake, I'm tied, and even if I weren't, I don't have the energy to even stand up. He sees me, opens the door, and sentences: "Don't follow me, you little shit, or I'll kill you and your entire family." And he leaves.

I struggle against my ties, but since they are plastic, little by little, my efforts at pulling end up stretching it, liberating me. I take off the gag, vomit twice, put on my bloodied clothes, and run after him, I don't really know why because I'm nine and can't really do much against an adult. Maybe, to see his face because I was never really able to? But Hurricane Hugo stops me in my tracks.

The door closes violently, but not before I am able to glimpse at where I am: a countryside that I had never seen before, full of the corpses of trees and sugar cane, and another corpse, a human one, pierced through by a plantain that must have been ripped from its tree, become a missile, and landed in an evil man's heart. The door slams too loud and too quickly. Somehow, the pressure of the winds outside keeps it sealed shut.

Inside the house where I am, I find a bathroom, I open the shower, and wash off the dried blood off my ass, and everything else, really. The question in my mind should be "What kind of man does this to a kid?" Instead, all I can think of is "what kind of man dies victim of a plantain missile?" I guess the same kind as women who abandon their family.

I dry off and wait until the storm passes. I must have dozed off because when I come back to it, I have drool all over my face and chest. Storm's over. And the door is wide open. No corpse in sight. No trees, no sugar cane. It's a big yellow nothing all around me and this house, all the way to the horizon. I start walking because, in times like this, it's always best to move. Even without a north.

The House of the Acerola Tree

My mother takes care of this old lady, Doña Ana, and my cousin and I will visit from time to time. Her house is one of those old Spanish revival atrocities that you can encounter in old urban developments that survive from the fifties. In fact, her house locates right in front of the residence of Walter Mercado, famous Puerto Rican astrologist, in Urbanización Villas de Cupey. Compared to the bright yellows, blues, and reds of the Starman's home, Doña Ana's house is also two-storied, but in a white that has seen better seasons, dirtied by the traces of roots from the old ivy creepers, and whose general aspect looks stagnant, withered, like the house of the old, one-eyed witch in *Big Fish*. No one young lives here, is the prevailing thought as soon as you see it. And you'd be right.

My cousin Pearl and I enter this house for the first time in 1992, when we are both twelve. The living room is saturated with the kind of armchairs and sofas and love seats that are so soft that, as soon as you sit, you are almost sucked into another dimension. Dangerous furniture, we both say at the same time. To the left is the kitchen and the door to the garage and the backyard, wherein lies the hidden treasure of this residence, something not even Walter Mercado's home has.

Back to the living room, it is possessed with wall-to-wall curios full to the brim of tacky porcelain figurines, like cats and dogs fixed in that retarded expression of longing, the object of such longing you could never simply identify, and the ballerinas covered in rhinestones, their faces defaced on purpose... it is a hellish parade of extreme bad taste, what with every single piece of furniture covered in that woven *macrame* in pastel pinks, blues, and yellows that screams old people.

The corridor leads to a room to the right that is always locked, a bathroom to the left, Doña Ana's room to the right, which contains her hospital bed, a TV set nailed to the wall, and her chest of drawers and closet. This is where the poor old lady spends most of her time, always connected to a dialysis machine. Doña Ana is nice and always receives us with cookies and two envelops with 5 dollars apiece, but she smells of urine, distant traces of shit, putrid fruit, dead flowers, and rubbing alcohol.

After Doña Ana's room, at the bottom of the corridor lies the master bedroom, all decorated in beige and wood. This was the bedroom of Doña Ana's daughter, Gladys, and the latter's husband Sean. Now, they both enjoy neutral colors in their clothes. Gladys is a fat woman who always wears silks. Silk pants, silk blouses, and silk panties. Sean sports a very long white beard, is thin and super tall. Something remains on his face of a past in which he must have been quite handsome. There is that amicable squint of his eyes when he smiles, and he does smile often. He always dresses in white or beige linens, and when he wears white linen pants, you can see the outline of his underwear.

Now, the TV room lies beyond the master bedroom, and that's where my mother leaves us, my cousin Pearl and I, to watch TV or play any of the boardgames we bring to entertain ourselves whenever we come to this house. There's *Candy Land*, *Monopoly*, and the *Ouija*, as well as all sorts of cards and jacks imaginable. After all, I have to spend every workday with mom for the entire summer. Pearl doesn't come every day to Doña Ana's with me, though. Only on Thursdays, because that's Auntie Estelle's day off from everything and everyone.

In the TV room, there's also the Cable TV, which Pearl and I adored, particularly VH1 and MTV. We would sit there for hours just watching videos and Rebecca Gayheart in her pop culture trivia program.

That first day at Doña Ana's, Mom goes to the TV room to tells us to come quickly to the backyard with her. Pearl and I follow her to the treasure: a dark acerola tree brimming with red berries.

Don't pick them up, yet. There are *aballardes* in there."

"*Aballardes*?" cousin Pearl asks.

"Tiny little red ants that bite hard. Here, let me just hose down the tree."

She grabs a green hose plugged to a wall faucet and opens. There is no nozzle, so Mom places her thumb the way you do in these cases if you want the water to come out with pressure, as a shower. Somehow, I see millions of *aballardes* falling to their deaths in the water streaming down and away into the earth. Pearl and I run to the tree and start by picking up those acerolas that have fallen, then working our way up the tree. When we're finished, we have three pails of paint full red berries.

"What's that?" I ask Mom, pointing to a very tiny wooden house at the back of Doña Ana's.

"That's where Dickie lives. You'll meet him tomorrow."

Next day, I go back to Doña Ana's with mom, sans Pearl. The acerola tree still has berries and I go pick some. A voice stops me.

"Leave some for the rest of us."

It comes from a brown-haired and eyed, tall white guy. He's dressed in a matching set of gray sweater and jogging pants.

"I'm Dickie," he says, coming closer to pick up some acerolas for himself. "Are you Molly's son?"

"Yes," I answer.

"I'll be using the TV room today. You can watch with me or play boardgames, but I'll be holding the remote."

His tone is matter-of-factly. I have nothing to say about it, so I shut up. We go back inside the house, Mom spots us, says "Oh, you met Dickie. Good. Go watch some TV together and stay out of my way," and scurries off to change Doña Ana's diaper. Dickie sits on the armchair, and I sit on the rugged floor. He turns on the TV set on the The Box channel. Jon Secada appears mid-video of his "Just Another Day." Then, along comes Guns N' Roses with its incomprehensible wedding video of "November Rain." Then, Michael Jackson with his go-happy-get-lucky "Black or White." Then, Madonna, with her hit "This used to Be my Playground," recorded for the movie *A League of Their Own*. Then, Mariah Carey with her gospel song "I'll be there." Music video after music video,

Dickie just keeps watching them with a weird face, sad eyes over a pursed and trembling mouth that says this is all life should be. This right here.

The Box has a novelty that no other music video channels have: a menu where you can choose the artist and music video you want next. You have to call, though, and enter the numbers corresponding to the music video you want. Dickie picks up the phone nonchalantly, enters a string of numbers and hangs up. We spend the rest of the afternoon watching his selection.

The next day, he's there too. This time, he's wearing jean cutoffs and a tank top. He makes several pauses watching his music videos in order to workout with dumbbells.

"Wanna try?" he asks, offering me a dumbbell.

I give it a go but it's so heavy that I am forced to grab it with both hands. I laugh as I give it back to him. He laughs too.

"Puny. No problem. You'll grow big."

We eat some acerolas and keep watching videos. Today, he doesn't call the channel. At some point, he stands up, tussles my hair, tells me to be good, and walks out, exits through the kitchen, goes to the backyard, and enters his little wooden apartment. He leaves the door open, and from the TV room's window, I watch as he peels off his cutoffs, adjusts his bulge over his tighty whities, grabs a beer from his mini fridge, and collapses on a white plastic chair to drink it. I take him all in with my eyes. It's Friday, so I probably won't see Dickie until next week.

On Monday, he's colonizing the TV remote all over again. Today, he's wearing dress slacks, moccasins, a white V-neck sweater. Today is Doña Ana's medical appointment, so Mom has to take her in her car.

"You're in charge, Dickie," my Mom sentences. "Be good."

"Yes, Molly. Promise."

"Do as Dickie says, Tony" she tells me.

"Do you want to see something interesting?" he asks when we reach the TV room.

"What?" I reply, curious.

"Come with me."

We go back to the master bedroom. Dickie opens Sean's underwear drawer to reveal a whole stash of full-cut white briefs, grandpa briefs as we call them at our school, from under which he grabs a VHS cassette with a golden sticker that read *Scoundrels*. He puts it in the VCR and hits play before sitting back on the armchair. The image of a very young Ron

Jeremy appears. He is dressed in 70s slacks and polyester shirt. A naked woman undresses him from behind. She takes off his shirt, pants, and white briefs. Then, the black-haired actress pries his ass open with her hands and delves tongue-first into his anus. This is the very first pornographic scene that I've seen in my life, and it will be engraved in my mind forever. I want it to stay with me forever.

The image of a man getting his chute eaten out by a woman sends my 11-year-old cock into frenzy. I get hard and cream right then and there. But I can't stop watching. And creaming. I turn to Dickie and see ooze coming out the front of his slacks. He catches me looking at his wet crotch. He smiles and then goes back to watch the movie.

"Take it out," he says. "Let me see it."

I take off my shorts and reveal a slimy little cock. "Dude, your Mom's gonna notice," he says. "You better go to the bathroom and wash that."

"How?"

"Come."

We go to the master bedroom's bathroom and he takes my briefs and shorts off, pours a lot of liquid hand soap, and starts scrubbing like his life depends on it. He washes both pieces thoroughly, wrings them out, and takes them to the drier.

"Sorry. I guess you'll have to stay like that for a while."

We go back to the TV room and this time he takes off his slacks. He is oozing like crazy and not caring that it is falling on the rug. His cock is short but thick and curved to the right.

"Wanna touch it?"

"Yes," I confess.

He grabs my hand and moves it toward his erect penis. It feels like one of those small exercise balls that people use to develop fine motor skills in children. As soon as I touch him, he creams, this time in my hand.

"I don't think I have any more of those in me," he says. "Here, let me have a go at you."

With some of his cream, he rubs the tip of my penis and plays with my foreskin. I spray immediately on his hand.

"Beautiful. Now, let me erase the evidence," he states, as he moves toward the VCR and hits *rewind*.

The next day, he is not home. Nor the next or the day after. In fact, he disappears for two of my summer weeks. I don't tell what happened to Pearl. She wouldn't understand.

But when I see the menu on the The Box channel, I pick up the phone and enter the necessary series of numbers. I spend those weeks watching whatever music videos I want. And every once in a while, when the adults are busy, I open Sean's underwear drawer and watch his flick.

My final week of summer, I go to Doña Ana's. Sean and Gladys are having a sit down with Dickie and it seems serious.

"Did you not think I would find out?" Gladys asks. She's livid. "Look at this telephone bill!"

"Just what did you buy with those $347, Dickie?" Sean interjects in a low, loving voice.

He doesn't answer. I'm watching everything from the window of the TV room.

"I want you gone by the end of the week," Gladys sentences and leaves. Dickie starts crying. Sean pulls him closer in a hug.

"How can you abandon me, daddy?"

"Shhh. She doesn't know. She thinks I took pity of an orphan and brought you in. She doesn't suspect anything. I'll talk to her. But this can't happen ever again."

Sean kisses Dickie in the mouth and enters the boy's wooden apartment behind the house. Sean touches Dickie's bulge and ass under his slacks, and Dickie kisses Sean's elderly neck.

But that's the last I see of Dickie. After the summer is over, Mom brings a black plastic bag full of clothes and asks me to try them on. There are pants, jeans, shorts, T-shirts, dress slacks, dress shirts, tighty whities, and bikinis (which are new to me).

"What's all this?"

"They were Dickie's. He won't be needing them anymore. Take what you like and leave the rest in the bag. Oh, and here."

She gives me a small bowl full of the red, orange, yellow, and green berries. Acerolas taste different depending on their ripeness stage. Green acerolas are sour to the extreme but refreshing. Yellow and orange acerolas taste sweeter, and the red ones are the sweetest of them all.

"I thought the season was over."

"Yup. These are the last ones. Make 'em last, baby."

It's Anatomy

    I listen to your fingers as they play the keys of the black Bösendorfer you love so much. We are at that hip bookstore with the hip barista girl with half her head shaved and the hip bookseller with her green and maroon dress shirt. We're supposed to be writing an opera in Spanish with two male and two female characters, and a dragon. Instead, I watch you play, imagining a life with you where I'd come home to you after work, and you'd start playing for me while I write for you. And right then and there, I want to kiss you, in front of everyone at the bookstore, without a care, and lower your pants, suck you off and ride your erection, right then and there, two men fucking in public out of that sheer unbridled force of new love that is almost impossible to understand, and yet we often do.

    And then you stop playing. You come back to our table.

    "So, how are we doing?"

    "I just wrote three pages," I say.

    "Good. Can I read?"

    And then you take my notebook, the one with the Celtic triquetra on its cover, and start reading. I drink you in, attempting to quench the unknown by just observing your scarcely square jaw, your thin body in that simple checkered long-sleeved shirt, and barely haired face, and that little hair at the edge of your left side of your beard that looked a bit too much like a pubic hair, but I say nothing. I keep tightening both my fists, trying not to jump on you. *You're too old for this, Genry*, I keep saying to myself, even though I'm barely 36 and not even close to a mirage of a midlife crisis.

"So, let me see if I get this straight: you want the dragon to be a god, and you want the Taino priestess to fall for him? That quick?"

"Sure. Why not?"

"This is good," you say, and I, Genry Izquierdo, fifteen years your senior, feel validated. "Although, now I'm getting all these ideas that I could add to it. How about this dragon cannot manifest himself in the physical plain unless he shares half of his soul with an intermediary human, in this case, the priestess?"

"Awesome. I like it. Let's do something: brainstorm part's over, so why don't we both go back to our homes and start working on it, then we exchange and consolidate our work?"

"We have a tight deadline."

"I know, but we can do this."

"Ok. Let's do it."

"Alright, then," I conclude. "I'll be seeing you."

"Wait. Where did you park your car?"

"I didn't."

"How did you arrive here?"

"My cousin brought me," I reply.

"And how are you getting back home?"

"I live close by. I'll walk."

"No, you won't. You're coming with me."

"Where to?"

"To places you've never been to," you say, and that's actually the point where I think you take possession of me.

"Ok, then." You open your car, and when I'm about to step in, I accidentally scrub the passenger's door against and bump on the sidewalk, and you say something like "Easy, does it," and I reply with a feeble "I'm sorry," because you've already put your leash around me and I'm your dog.

So, we drive to Old San Juan, but I convince you to go instead to the park in front of the Supreme Court in Puerta de Tierra. We step off your car.

"What's that structure over there?" you ask, referring to an old sort of fortification in the park itself that, according to you, looks as if Gaudí had left one of his cupcakes in Puerto Rico, and now that I think of it, yeah, it looks like that. We climb the stairs, and on top of the wee fort there we find chairs and two watch turrets. We sit there for a while.

"Do you come here often?" you ask.

"Every afternoon," I lie. "I come here to get away from it all. At lunch time."

"You are so fortunate."

"I guess I am."

You start getting your paraphernalia out of your knapsack. You want to roll a joint, until I stop you.

"Let's go to the beach. Come on. I'll show you a special place."

You put everything back in again and we start towards the bridge that crosses over the highway in order to get to El Escambrón, that ever-mutable beach that is often a serene lake during the day and a furious creature at night. We pass over the baseball field that is being used that night for a teen American football practice.

"Go figure," I say, meaning that so many un-Puerto Rican things have been arriving lately to the island, American football the most recent, but you miss that, I guess.

We keep walking towards the beach, all the while climbing a small slope that leads to the most furious wave crashing part of El Escambrón, where rocks part ways with the sand and embrace the fierce salute of the salty water. Three pillars of something that must have been an ancient pier still stand to this day, being devoured by the rusting action of the ocean an inch each decade, because if there is something true about this world is that everything rusts away in due time.

We sit there, under some cover of the *Coccoloba* bushes and a wee palm tree. You roll your joint while I illuminate you with your cell phone torch. You lick the end of the paper and seal it with your lighter. Then, you explain the rules of puffing, first one being "The person who rolls is the one who lights and puffs first," and I acquiesce because that's all I can do at this point: say "yes" to everything you say, because you have owned me from the Bösendorfer.

Smoking under the veil of the full moon makes me feel ridiculous for a bit, but I recover at the second puff, and I keep smiling your way as you tell me that idea for a story that you had, the one about when a person dies her consciousness shatters and all the fragments are thrown into outer space, and when a person is born, a fragment of the consciousness of each person alive and dead joins in a conglomerate that will form that individual's personality. I think it's beautiful.

"Pity that we're a hive mind, though," you say.

"Pity that we don't know it," I reply.

You smile at me and then go on to state just how glad you are that I have a brain, unlike most of the people you know and have to interact with. You, flatterer, you. Then, I softly caress your face, going from the sparse scruff and moustache to your hair in that hipster haircut that I love so much, sort of a modernized, polished flock of seagulls. You make like a cat and rub your face against my hand. That's when I grow hard. I want to rip your clothes off and possess you right there. But you're in charge and deep in my cerebellum I have accepted my doom. I pull you close, and we share a deep kiss.

You don't stick your tongue in me, at first. You wait for me to do it. You, gentleman, you. You want me to lead, to be the older guy you need me to be. So, I lead you in our tongue dance, imagining all the time that we're dragons and that mortals sing of us in bitter Spanish operas, and that this moment could stay ageless, robbed of any decay, frozen in the flux of facts, events, questions, and importance. An exemplary kiss, befitting the literary.

I lay on the grass and pull you on top of me, and the kiss gravitates towards a deeper touch as we caress and remove our clothes, all the way rubbing against each other's crotch. I feel your erection and you feel my beating thing. A thought occurs to me. *Don't tell him you love him. Enjoy this as the mirage it is. You have a husband, he has a boyfriend. See this through, but don't cross the line.* Yet the kiss invites me to love you, and so I do. I love you right then and there, as I nibble and suckle at your left nipple and remove your belt. Suddenly, we have rolled, and I am on top of you, removing your pants and your gray boxer briefs. I take your cock in my mouth and suck it to the very base, because this way, somehow, I will drink you in, and the more I do, the more this moment will last even after it's gone.

As I continue sucking you off, I notice the curvature of your cock. Hard as it is, it looks like an arch, climbing three inches and then falling five or six more to half an inch of foreskin. I pull it back and suck, push it forth and play with it, imagining your dick to be a Bösendorfer, each crease of your foreskin a key, my action a symphony for the full moon beneath the clouds. Suddenly, I push a finger in your hairy ass, and you squirm, but then moan. You like it. I hit your hidden, pulsating egg, and keep sucking you, until I just need you inside. So, I step off a bit, pull down my pants and underwear, and just stay on fours, waiting for your thrust.

I know it will hurt. I want it to. As I brace myself, you appease my fears with your tongue. You don't stick in this time but play with my ring. I know you do it this way to see if you can get a symphony of moans out of me. You do. And then, you stick it in. I am so high on weed that all I can feel as an intense burn. *Gee, Genry, you're not an amateur, for chrissakes*, I tell myself, and I grab my ass cheeks with both hands and pry them apart, allowing you to stick your entire manhood in me in one go. It's then that I lose. You have me. I am your dog, your beast, and you're riding me. Taming me. I need to be tamed. You plunge hard and I know I will bleed and can't care less. You fuck me, every thrust deeper and harder, every withdrawal longer, until I go so nuts that I impale myself against your pole, because somehow, I want to be made whole by you, to be a hive with you, to share more than a mere moment, but an entire lifetime imagined in a single second, an imagination that will perhaps create an alternate reality I can glimpse every time I have a déjà vu. I keep fucking myself against you, proving to you that I am yours even if I don't want to say it, to put it in words, for fear that it will make it certain and force us to do something about it, leave our partners and embark together in a forbidden quest that will destroy us four. I keep silent, save for the occasional rhythmic moan, until I come. Anally.

I feel a pulse in my ring. My prostate protests under the heavy fire. But you keep at it, until I feel you will fuck your whole body into me, my hole becoming a black star. Then, I come harder, my prostate telling me to say the words that need to be said.

"Give it to me, please."
"You want it?"
"Yeah, give it to me."

And twenty or thirty thrusts later, my head already spinning, you come inside, flushing my guts with your own pulsations. You withdraw, I incorporate myself and jack off while you caress my butt and chest. I guide your finger towards my ass, and you understand, thrusting your thumb in, until I start gasping for air and shooting my load. It is over, yet we kiss again. It can't be over. Not now. But it is. Now everything left is a remembrance of air, crashing waves, an idiotic moon, and two friends turned lovers turned friends again by the memory of duty towards our partners. I want to cry because I have crossed over to the alternate reality and seen wonders. I have seen us married, with two dogs and two cats. You playing piano every afternoon after I come back from work, and me writing, inspired by your music. We will fuck each other's brains every day and you will tell me you love me and that there is no love more powerful ever professed, because ours is the perfect combination of all the fragments of this planet's hive mind that relate to love. I am shocked and wonder whether I can collect my shattered self in a dignified way and ask you to take me home. I wonder whether I can look at my husband in the face and tell myself that everything is alright, that it has all been mere meaningful sex.

"That was awesome," I say.

"What can I say?" you reply. "It's anatomy."

Fucker. You brand those words in my brain and all hope to let it all be meaningless is tossed into the breeze.

While we walk back to your car, I ask you to hold my hand.

"Why?" you ask.

"I want to know what it feels like."

"Why? You've never held hands with your husband in public before?"

"Sure. I just want to know what it feels like to do it with you."

And as you hold my hand, half of my soul crosses over. The other half says goodbye.

WarGod Beach Romance

"Don't you think it's a bit too crowded?" you ask.

"Nah. It'll be fine. We'll have a great time."

We enter the jungle in Itanam'izen, that old forest town at the north of the island. I park the car at the left side of the trail, as the paved street had led, several miles ago, to a beaten road, trampled dirt that will spell trouble if the sky decides to fall on us. We step out of the vehicle and look at the forest, seeking the sound of the sea.

"I can hear voices," you say.

"Yup. There must be a school bus full of brats somewhere."

The cackles increased in volume as we approach the jungle. The voices are carried by the subtle breeze, as even the tiniest space between the trees let a blessing of cold air through. This land is benevolent.

We take a left at some point, following a trail that many *someones* had left before. I grab your hand, as the path is slippery. We have to climb some narrow rocks that cross a dirty mangrove. I'm afraid I'll slip and soil my clothes. You grab my ass and direct me from behind. That's one of the coolest things about you: even though you are a skinny boy in your twenties, you still manage to know when to take control and prevent my fall. I look at you and we kiss. A jungle kiss, I joke. You laugh. We're happy.

The path leads to an open clear that is obviously used by vehicles. The tracks are fresh, and we follow.

"We must be close," I say. "I remember this."

"How long ago did you come here?"

"Five or six years?"

"Erosion must be accounted for."

You are right. I miscalculate, take the wrong turn, and must back up a bit, take the entrance to the right and keep going, all the while trying to remember details of the road I'm taking.

"It's easier if we follow the sound of the sea," you sentence, and of course, you're right, and I should have listened to you. Instead, we end up in the public area of the beach, the family side.

"Urgh. I hate family beaches," I declare.

You nod.

The water looks murky and brown, as if myriads of people had used it as a toilet. Beyond to the right, we see several dozen teenagers. We stay under the bushes, surveying the area. There are like forty or fifty imps screaming, fucking, playing, throwing sand at each other's eyes, and finally, fighting. A guy in a black T-shirt slams a crystal bottle against another's skull, landing the latter face front to the sand. The victim faints and his brother starts punching the guy in the black T-shirt. All those who are screaming, fucking, playing, and throwing sand at each other's eyes stop whatever they're doing and join in a circle around the combatants. Some cheer the brother, the others the guy in the black T-shirt, while the least enthusiastic try to grab the one on the sand, the one who has fallen face front, beaten, humiliated, diminished.

I grab your hand, and we're gone by the time the student stampede starts. We take the long road to the left, around the jungle that surrounds the most secluded beaches in Itanam'izen. At some point, you stop me, kiss me again, and let me have some air.

"I'm getting old," I pant.

"Nonsense," you reply, and those black eyes of yours shine like the last drops of petrol in a world with no gas to go on.

"What if I wanted to make love to you, right here and now?"

"I'm shy in public spaces."

"Why? We've done it before on a beach."

"Yeah, it was dark and there was no one around."

"Fair enough."

"Fair enough," you repeat and you make that face gesture like "yeah, you got that right, I'm right on this one" that makes me smile and hold your hand again.

When we finally emerge, I think we're on the wrong beach. To our right, a young couple shares a moment, naked, under the glaring sun. She is naked. He isn't, but all the same, they are making love, unfazed by the heat or the possibility of being discovered. We turn left to where we find several giant WarGod statues, those totems invented during the 22nd Century when we attempted to harness the power of the forgotten magic of this world and channel it through guardians that would defend the island against incoming missiles from the United States Mecha Marine. The WarGods are rusty, even though they're made of stainless steel. I touch one as we pass it by. The glyphs shine bright, even under the sun, and just as quickly shut down.

"Don't touch that, Richter. You don't want them to come alive."

"Oh, you sourpuss," I reply and we laugh. *Sourpuss* is a word from earlier centuries. No one uses it anymore, and it goes to highlight my age when compared to yours. I am reaching my forties and you are barely twenty. To tell you the truth, I have never really understood what you see in me. I am not fit anymore. I have taken a magi bullet in both legs, and though I recover with some *Curaga* spell the doctors try, the bullet's still there, and I can't run or pretty much do any exercise. I am chubby and feel the weight of years of unending war on my body. The War of the Lights, they call it. The light of the spells as they crash against, slash, and burn flesh, wood, metal, and stone all the same. The War had lasted the entire century and we had not come off better humans after it. An entire 105 years of airships, levitating humans, WarGods, familiars... all lost just as quickly as they arose.

"You're lost in thought," you interrupt. "Come back to me." You wrap your arms around my neck and beg me to let you ride me.

"Piggyback? Really, Gabe?

"Why not? You're soooooo strong!"

"Right..." I become serious, brooding, and silent, and you respect that. We come to a spot where a couple of young men are having sex under the shadow of a rusty guardian. I become hard immediately and want us to join them, but you keep walking. Later on, I ask you why, but you can't give me a reason, so I let it be.

As we press on, the sand becomes too loose, and every step employs a force and an energy that we're quickly losing. We pass a man chubbier and older than I. He's erect and has all sort of cockrings on. As if doubling the magic will actually work on him.

Finally, we make a final turn to the left and discover an eye of water, a special corner where the bay becomes beach, jungle, and river all at the same time. We put our backpacks on the sand and you start rolling a puffer.

"You're gonna love this weed," you sentence.

"Where's it from?" I inquire.

"All the way from the farthest fjords of Norway."

"Are you serious? Just how the fuck did you get your hands on that in Nuevo Puerto Rico?"

"I've connections," you reply.

And I think *this is the guy I'd like to marry*. A young man full of surprises. A beautiful prince of a man. While you get the joint ready, I take off my clothes, place my cockring on, and put on a grey and purple swimmer. You look at me, lost in those pervy adolescent eyes I've come to adore.

"Do you like what you see?" I ask.

"Very much so, yes," and I notice you're hard under your jeans.

"Come here." I pull you close, kiss you full in the mouth, and put a hand on your ass. I take off your shirt and kiss your neck, nibble at your nipples, smell and tongue your hairy armpits, and gobble your navel. I pull down your pants and start sucking you off. Your member makes an arch as it strives for the sky yet falls down in the attempt. I name it Icarus. I suckle at it, until you tell me you don't want to be naked anymore. I look around and the old man we had passed before is all erect, a hundred meters from us, give or take, stroking to the horizon. I confess I want him to join us, but as you shy away like a puppy warg, I give you the other swimmer, the white and turquoise one. You put it on, and I swear you look like one of those 21st Century Brazilian men in their *sungas*.

"I've never worn one of these."
"Don't you like them?"
"I feel uneasy."
"Would you rather be naked?"
"No."
"You look gorgeous. A true prince. My prince."

We kiss again and I feel some drops of water on my skin. At first, I think it should have been the breeze carrying some of the foamy water onto our skins. We smoke the puffer together, embracing each other, basking in each other's presence. There will be hell to pay if one of us has an accident while being here, I think. You have a boyfriend, and I am engaged to another man. But there's an understanding between us. We're always honest to each other. We talk about our partners and how much we love them, then kiss and have sex, then smoke, then talk about them again and how much we love them. You say once that we're two adults who enjoy each other's company and that there's naught wrong with that. I let go and slip a finger in your ass while we kiss. You jump but don't squirm and I am thankful that you're clean. You're always clean. So fucking clean. You follow suit and penetrate me with two fingers. Then you take them to your mouth and suck an imaginary honey and slip back into me. We kiss and finger fuck each other until we can't hold it any longer.

"I want to be your daddy," I say out of impulse.

"Ok," you reply, and thrust your pole into me, impaling me on the sand. The weed is good, and I can feel the magic of the land escaping the glyphs and cursing blue and white and green through my veins. I am the sun hidden. I am the clouds dark. I am the beach untamed. The waves quiet. The forest hungry. The jungle at peace. The WarGods silent. The glyphs in me. I erupt. You do too, inside me.

"You're mine now, daddy," you say.

I don't reply. There's another understanding. We love each other and no words are necessary to get that. We just know.

You force me on fours, on the sand, pry by butt apart with your hands and carefully guide mine so I stay like that for you, ass up, face down, dinner is served. You eat me up and then fuck me all the way to my stomach. I cry of pure, sheer, unbridled joy. My final anal spasm makes me reach with my hand, and unwittingly, I touch one of the WarGods.

And then we feel it. The tremors, the powerful bots shifting in their sleep, letting go of centuries of rust, recuperating their pristine qualities by sucking the aura off the air. The giants move, a finger here, a tic of the eye yonder. The couples who have been fucking leave in a hurry, stumbling upon such loose sand. The giants glow with the power of the glyphs: myriads concentric circles with runes and eldritch symbols written all over and around, in gold, silver, copper, and cobalt, all shimmering as the war spells charge up.

A star twinkles hard, and suddenly, a creature stands on the waters as tall as Queen Sky herself, a gargantuan green fox with deer antlers all covered in moss and leaves and stars and fairy spells. The WarGods stand no chance, but still, they ready their gamma rays, nuclear needle, and holy radiance attacks. All projectiles are absorbed by the Deerfox StarGod. That's when I pull you up and bid you to hide with me among the trees.

"Are we gonna die?" you ask.

"No," is all I say while I look at you with red concerned eyes.

I turn my eyes back to the battle, the machines spent, their centuries old magi energy gone, and the StarGod just standing there. Seizing us up. I dare not look at it anymore, and so we embrace and await judgment. Together.

Instead, the creature lifts us with its many beautiful silk tentacles, gossamer things that carry us gently onto its back. Then, it guides us out of the forest, back to the parking lot, where we stand naked, drenched in each other's urine, still embraced in a trembling bundle of survivors' joy. We put on our clothes nervously and drive back to the capital, all the while thinking of the bullet we just dodged.

Contents

Preface 3
Hair 8
The Jesus Man 23
An Embrace From a Beautiful Stranger Who Drowned Forever 33
How to Turn Into a Faeling 46
The English Teacher 52
The Unsolvable Problem 62
Plop! 67
A Month with James Franco 82
Antiaris toxicaria var. ultimata 97
Freaky Bloody Katana 107
Isentress 132
Old Man Nereus 152
Tarot for Writers 163
The Floating Church 187
The Mutherfuckin- Trans Everest 201
The Map She Etched in My Head 212
The Shelter Thus Becomes the Tomb .. 225
Katayama Fever 228
Our Love Is Like Anime 241
Peter Frampton's Guitar Gently Weeps 254
Thunderclap 266
Even Without a North 275
The House of the Acerola Tree 281
It's Anatomy 292
WarGod Beach Romance 302

The following individuals read and proofed this manuscript:

Yahmái Flores Pérez, writer, editor, and content creator for educational books.

Rosalina Martínez González, writer, editor, translator, and author of the poetry book *Cadáver de bailarina / Corpse Ballerina*.

Eïrïc R. Durändal Stormcrow is born in San Juan, Puerto Rico, in 1980. Writer and visual artista, he has published poetry: *Bestiario en nomenclatura binomial, Empírea: Saga de la Nueva Ciudad, Pie forzado, Terrarium, Hustler Rave XXX: Poetry of the Eternal Survivor* (with Charlie Vázquez), *Niños malcriados / Rotten Children, La honra del Jabberwöck / The Honour of the Jabberwöck, the Williwaw of Frank Mathis / the Williwaw* y *Tribu de los vientos / Skyward Tribe*; novels: *el Oneronauta* and *Historias para pasar el fin del mundo*; books of stories: *Desongberd, Las formas del diablo, Cielos negros / Skies Blackened, Biografía de los planetas tristes / Biography of the Planets in Sorrow, Puto noviembre / Fuck November*, and *El Evangelio del Fénix*; the sexposé *Diario de una puta humilde*; the travel chronicle *Crónicas del esmog*, and anthologies: *Los otros cuerpos: antología de literatura gay, lésbica y queer desde Puerto Rico y su diáspora* (with Moisés Agosto Rosario y Luis Negrón), *Felina: antología para gatos* (with Cindy Jiménez-Vera), *Fricción cuántica: antología de ciencia ficción desde Puerto Rico y su diáspora*, and *Antología de cuentos pornoeróticos de Gnavidad*.

This book was published in June 2023, in Puerto Rico, a country victim of the horrors of the Financial Oversight and Management Board, Trump and his indolent empire, a local administration characterized by neglect, theft, corruption and theft of public funds, an undeclared civil war towards women and the LGBTQ+ community, two category 5 hurricanes, the tremors and earthquakes that began on Three Kings Day, a pandemic empowered and enabled by all of the above, and a stolen election, along with our future. In the face of such a bleak outlook, may literature serve as an escape, a northstar, and a salvation.

GNOMO

San Juan, Puerto Rico

Made in the USA
Columbia, SC
09 July 2023